A Rift in Time

Clark Graham

Cover Artwork by JJ. Schutza

elvenshore.blogspot.com

elvenshore@gmail.com

A Rift in Time

Time Loop Series

Book One

A Loop in Time

Book Two

A Hole in Time

Book Three

A Rift in Time

Contents

Chapter One

"She's down there all right. It's a plane, but like no plane I've seen before. No propeller and only one wing on the bottom. The upper wing either tore off or it never had one." The captain smiled, showing his chewing tobacco stained teeth. His blue cap was weather worn and sweat-stained. Scratching his grey stubby beard, he continued. "I had to get a bigger crane. This machine of yours was larger than I expected. We're ready to pull her up. All you got to do is say the word."

"An airplane. Of course." Ted smiled. "He was traveling when he lost it. That explains how he was stuck out in the ocean. How did you find it?"

"I took the captain's log of the *Wilhelm*. It was the ship that picked him up. It took me a long time to figure that out, though where it was though. The crew was interred because they were in New York City when our country entered the war. The logs and all the papers were saved in the City Library. I read where the ship was when they found a survivor in the water. It was still a large area to search, but I caught a break when I saw a clam dredge boat alter its course, then go back on the course it was on. I talked to the captain later on, at a tavern. He told me there was something on the bottom there, so he goes around it. He's lost gear there before. I figured that's where it was, the machine you were wanting."

"Good work, bring her up."

The crane's hook splashed down into the water at the captain's signal. Two divers, in large diving suits with hoses attached, soon followed. The process was tedious. A diver would be brought to the surface after an hour and another one took his place. A man would be exhausted after being in the suit for long periods of time. When rested, he would go back in and another would come up to take a break. They repeated this every hour.

The two barges were lashed together with long timbers, leaving a gap between them. The crane was positioned on one barge they were going to put the time machine on the other.

The project was halted at nightfall, but early in the morning, the men were at it again. When the plane was finally secured to the crane's hook, the massive yellow crane came to life. Steam and smoke came billowing out. The cables tightened and wound up slowly.

Ted could see the shape of the craft under the water as it neared the surface. He was like a boy in a candy store. The time machine would soon be his to play with.

As part of the plane cleared the surface, the captain came up to him. "Here's the hard part. Instead of moving the thing over onto the other barge, I'm going to pick it straight up and move the barge under it. Less chance of the crane tipping over that way."

"Good idea."

As the plane broke the surface, Fishing nets and ropes hanging from it. Ted's enthusiasm waned. The thing was in a lot worse shape than he'd supposed. Seaweed and barnacles were all over the craft. Parts of it were broken and bent too. His heart sank.

The crane strained to hold the plane in place. The timbers were untied and a tug pushed the second barge under the time machine. Slowly, the battered time machine was set down on the barge. After tying the plane up, the tug locked on to both barges and began towing them back to New York. Ted and the captain followed in the dive ship.

It was as if the captain read Ted's thoughts. "Things always look bad when you first pull them from the water. I'll get her cleaned up for you. It'll be better, you'll see."

Ted nodded. "Yes, it does look bad, but I don't much care for what it looks like. I need the thing to work. It doesn't look like it ever will."

"That, I can't help you with."

When the tug pulled up to the pier a few days later, the plane was unloaded into one of the bays of a warehouse. Ted had it leased. The salvage company took on the painstaking task of cleaning the wreckage. They chipped off all of the barnacles, pulled out all of the seaweed, marine growth, and silt.

After months of work, they called Ted in to look at the project.

The captain, still in his blue stained cap, pointed out several things he had discovered. "It looks like there were two motors. One over the other. I don't know why, but they are different types." Pointing at the landing gear he continued, "We were able to deploy those. They were tucked up inside the body. The tires have rotted away. At least we think they had rubber on them at some time."

He moved to the front of the plane. Ted looked up. "Two seats?"

"Different controls." The captain brought Ted around to the side where his men had built a staircase up to the cockpit. "The controls in the back controls the time machine. It has month, day, year, settings. It was set for May 5, 2035. The other controls, in the front flies the plane. This is a time machine, only, we don't know how to run it. Are you going to ask your friend for help? I mean, the guy that flew on this thing?"

"No, he must never know we found it. I'll bring in experts, maybe they can figure it out."

Chapter Two

New York City, New York
1925

A scaffolding erected over the airplane had a half dozen men inspecting every square inch of the time machine. They had disassembled and reassembled every part, taking pictures as they did. Another man walked around jotting down notes.

A panel was removed and everything behind it would be layed out on a table, photographed, and then put back. All Ted could see was stacks and stacks of photos and documents. The bills were adding up, too, rent on the warehouse, not to mention the men's salary.

He tried on several occasions to talk to the man in charge, only to get snapped at. "We are not done. You'll have to wait for the final report."

These men were expert in the fields of aeronautics and engineering. If they couldn't figure out how the thing worked and what it was going to take to fix it, nobody could.

A month and a half later, the completed report sat in front of him. "Well, give me the short version. I'm not going to read a thousand pages of engineering mumbo jumbo which I probably wouldn't understand anyway."

Lawrence Hardy's face flashed red for just a second before the man regained control. Ted could tell he didn't like talking to people he considered inferior to him. Lawrence was a total introvert in Ted's eyes.

"Well, the report details out how to put this thing together and where every part goes and their relationship to other parts. The plane was under water a long time and a lot of the aluminum parts are corroded. They will have to be replaced. The ailerons and spoilers are run by hydraulics, but that system is contaminated. Those components will have to be taken out, too. Most of the wires run along…"

"I don't care about where the parts go," Ted interrupted. "I want you to tell me how to fix it."

Lawrence took a deep breath, then started in, talking really slow. "That's the hard part. We know what most of the parts are, but have never seen some of them. The green boards in the electrical boxes are a mystery to us. I can tell you what happened. The oil tank was shot up. When the engine ran out of oil, I'm talking about the top engine, it seized up. The other engine is more intact, except for hitting the water at a high speed. It ran out of gas. These engines are so far advanced from the technology of today, that the ideas behind them have not been thought of yet."

"You can't fix it?"

Lawrence shook his head slowly back and forth. "No, we don't have the technology to fix this thing."

Ted glared at him. "All that money I paid you and you can't deliver?"

"You paid for my services." Lawrence glared back. "I provided those services. I went over this thing with a fine-tooth comb. It's all there in the report. We now know so much about it, but we don't have the technology to fix something from the next century." He turned and walked out without another word.

Ted walked around the machine. "What are your secrets and how do I get them from you?" He walked over and grabbed the phone receiver. After dialing a number, he said, "Those guys couldn't help me. It's your turn to try."

"I'll see you in a few hours, Ted."

The same story played out again. They looked over the report from the previous attempt, then pulled the thing apart and put it back together. Jay, the man in charge of the team, wasn't a report writer. He pulled a couple of parts out and brought them over to Ted. "I can't fix it until you can tell me what these are."

Jay held out two green circuit cards.

"You're the expert," Ted snapped.

"I've seen hundreds of planes, some with dead bodies in them. I've been to my share of crashes and I've pieced planes back together that were in a million pieces, but I've never seen anything like this and nobody else has either. If you can tell me what they do and how to fix them, I might be able to get this thing running again."

Ted studied them. "I'll find out, then I'll get you back here. Meanwhile, you and your men can take a break until you hear from me."

Chapter Three

New York City, New York
1947

Ted sat across from Dr. Rendahl of New York University. He had watched the doctor look at the panel he brought him, scratch his head, and then look at it again.

"I can't even guess what this thing does. It's so small, but it has a lot of pieces to it. They're glued together somehow. I can't help you, Sir. I'm truly sorry." He handed the part back to Ted.

Ted nodded and left. It had been over two decades and still he couldn't figure out how the machine worked, or even what it did.

There was still one man he hadn't asked after all these years. Dalton had been sick lately, so Ted thought he would finally risk it. He called Mary. She said he could come by for a visit.

He drove out to the house. Mary answered the door. She wasn't smiling. Her lovely red hair was now grey. "Hello, Ted."

"How's he doing?"

She shook her head. "He keeps telling the doctors how to cure him, but he names procedures that haven't been invented yet. They stare at him dumbfounded."

"I see. Is he up to visitors?"

"Yes, he would love to see you."

She escorted him to the back bedroom where Dalton lay. He smiled when he saw Ted. "It's been a long time. How are you doing, Ted?"

"Great, Adalwolf. You've been better, I hear."

"Those doctors won't listen. I'm dying of prostate cancer. It would be easily cured if I was back in my own time."

"That's what I've come to talk to you about." Ted handed him a panel from the plane. "I've got it. I pulled up the time machine. We can get you back to your time and fix you."

Dalton's eyes widened. "No. Destroy it. It will be the end of the world if you use it. Promise me you'll destroy it."

Ted shook his head violently. "We have to get you back to save you. Don't you understand?"

Grabbing his arm, Dalton looked him in the eye. "I let a little boy die. Just one little boy. When I came back to my own time, the timeline was destroyed. One little boy. I went back and saved him. Using that machine will cause catastrophic results. Destroy it. I'd rather die than have that machine available for someone to use."

Ted stared at him for the longest time. "You mean that, don't you?"

"Yes, please, get rid of it."

"I promise."

Dalton took a deep breath. "Thank you. I know you think you want to see the future, but you don't. What if I had told you about the two world wars that first day I met you. Millions of people were going to die and all you could do is sit and watch. The horrors and joy of life will get here when they get here."

"I suppose you're right. I wanted a peek. I wanted to know what to invest in. You've made millions. I wanted that for me."

"I know, but even if I wanted to, I couldn't fix that machine. The parts to repair it haven't been invented yet. That will come many years from now. You'll be dead before then."

"Good to know, old friend. I must be going."

"Take care."

Ted gave him one last look before showing himself out.

As soon as he left, Dalton turned to Mary. "I want to see Bryan."

"I'll call him."

Bryan had his mother's red hair. He stood six foot and had a slight limp. He'd been hit by shrapnel during the war while captaining a freighter in the merchant marine. His mother and father had begged him not to go to war, but he felt he had to do his part.

Standing over the bedside, Bryan asked, "What is it, Father?"

"Ted found the time machine. He promised to destroy it, I want you to make sure he does."

"I'll make sure of it."

That hadn't gone to plan. Ted ground his teeth as he drove away. He wanted help, not a lecture. He was deep in thought as he drove. *Am I really going to destroy it like he promised, after spending a lot of money to get it?* His emotions were still high when he turned onto the main road to New York City. He didn't see the truck. It couldn't stop.

Ted's car was cut in two by the force of the collision. He died instantly.

Chapter Four

New York City, New York
1948

There's that bill again. What was my father doing, renting a warehouse at the wharf? Mel sat at his desk going through his father's affairs. It had been six months since the funeral and he was still trying to clean up the paperwork.

Jotting down the address, he decided to drive out there and figure out what was going on. When he arrived, he was stopped at the gate.

"State your business." The armed guard was abrupt.

"My father was renting unit number 5 when he passed away. He. I need to see what's in there."

"Papers." The guard's expression didn't change. The brown eyes seemed to cut through the darkness.

"I don't know what type of papers you mean."

"I can't let you in then." The guard walked away before Mel could respond.

When he arrived back at his father's house, he tore the place apart. Finally, in an overcoat, he found a key and some papers with the letterhead of the wharf printed on it. It was too late to go back, so he slept on the couch and waited for the new day.

At the pier, a different guard looked over the papers, then nodded and opened the gate. Mel drove up to the door of the warehouse. Trying the key, he had a hard time unlocking it. Something was stuck. He shook the door. That did the trick.

In the center of the building, a large object was covered in tarps. He pulled them back to reveal the airplane. "Wow." He walked around, admiring it. He had never seen one so large before. It was a new one without propellers, yet it looked very old and weathered.

This has to be worth millions. A smile creased his lips. He covered it back up, and drove to his father's place. He knew there had to be more information on it. His father kept meticulous records. Tearing the house apart again, he found nothing.

An idea occurred to him. He called his father's lawyer. "Howard, this is Mel. Listen, I keep getting a bill for a wharf on the waterfront."

There was a pause. "That bill was supposed to come to me. Don't pay it, I'll handle it."

"So, you do know about it then."

"Know about what?"

Mel shook his head. "Don't play stupid, Howard, it doesn't suit you. You know about the plane in the warehouse. The one I went and took a look at this morning."

Another long pause. "Yes, I know. I wish I didn't. That thing has been nothing but a thorn in my side since your father pulled it from the ocean floor. I now have the estate of Adalwolf Dalton breathing down my neck. They want it so they can destroy it. Trust me, you'd be better off forgetting it existed."

"What is it?"

"Some apocalyptic device, according to the Daltons. They don't know where it's at and I mean to keep it that way. I've got to go. Send me the bill. I'll handle it."

The phone went dead. Instead of feeling intimidated, Mel was more intrigued. Going through his father's address book, he looked up Adalwolf Dalton.

Two hours later, he sat in his car across the street from the Dalton home. He debated what to do. He couldn't just ask what it was. *I've found the machine, what does it do?* Finally getting up his nerve, he went up to the front door and knocked.

An older woman answered the door. "May I help you?"

"I'm here to see Adalwolf Dalton."

"You're too late. He passed away three months ago."

"Oh." Mel let out a sigh. "I'm sorry to have bothered you in your time of mourning."

"May I ask who you are?"

"I'm Mel. My father was Ted."

She put her hands over her mouth. "Ted's son. My, oh, my." She looked both ways. "Did you destroy it?"

"Destroy what?" He played stupid in hopes of getting an answer.

"That time machine. Did you destroy it?"

"Oh that, of course. It was my father's will that it be destroyed."

"Thank goodness."

Bryan listened to the conversation from around the corner. He cringed when his mother mentioned the time machine. A few moments later his blood ran cold. He had been in business long enough to know when someone was lying, and this man wasn't good at it.

Waiting until Mel left, he walked up to his mother. "Who was that?"

"That was Ted's son. The time machine has been destroyed."

"Father would have been happy to hear it."

Chapter Five

New York Harbor
1948

Mel smiled to himself. *A time machine! I can control the world with one of these.* He needed more information. His father was a meticulous record keeper. There had to be more information on the plane somewhere. It wasn't at home, he knew that for a fact. It had to be somewhere in the warehouse.

The next day he drove down to the pier. He scanned the room. There was a table full of tools, and time machine parts, but nothing else. He pulled the tarp off of it and set a ladder against it. Looking in the cockpit, he saw boxes, upon boxes on the seats and sitting in the storage area behind them. *Aha.*

"For a machine that was destroyed, it looks very intact to me." The voice came from behind him.

Mel whirled his head around. "Who are you?"

"Bryan Dalton. You told my mother you destroyed this thing. You lied."

"How did you find me?"

"You sent the bill for the warehouse to your lawyer to pay."

"Yes, and so what?"

Dalton smiled. "He's also my lawyer. He let me know where the plane was as soon as the bill arrived. I have a barge waiting and a lot of dynamite. I'm putting it on the barge, taking it out to sea and blowing it sky high. I wasn't expecting to see you here today though."

Mel climbed down from the ladder. "You can't do that. It's mine."

Bryan held up a piece of paper. "Our lawyer has given it over to me because it was my father's originally. I have every right."

Mel grabbed the paper from his hand and read it. "He's fired."

"He won't care. I pay him a lot better than you pay him."

Panicking inside, Mel still kept a calm face. "I'll fight this in the courts."

"You'll be too late. The barge arrives tomorrow. All I have to do is tell them where to park it, and they'll load up the plane. By the time you get a new lawyer, the plane will be in thousands of pieces."

Mel raged inside. It was as if he could feel the millions of dollars that he was losing. Grabbing a crowbar, he struck Dalton across the head. He hadn't meant to hit him that hard. Blood flowed out of the wound. Dalton collapsed to the floor, dead.

Pacing back and forth, Mel tried to figure out what to do. He tied most of the heavy tools, wrenches and crowbars, around Bryan's body, then waiting for midnight, he dragged Dalton to the edge of the pier and threw him in. As he walked towards the gate, he noticed another car parked next to his. *Oh, no. Dalton's car.* He couldn't leave it there. He looked inside, the key wasn't there. *It's in his pocket.* Mel shook his head. Why hadn't he looked there first? *Hotwire it.* As a child, he and a neighbor kid had stolen Ted's car. They only took it for an hour, then returned it. The neighbor kid had shown Mel how to hotwire.

He pulled the wires out and then stuck them together. The car started. He drove it several miles away, parked it in an industrial area, then walked back to the pier. It was nearly dawn when he arrived. He scrubbed the blood off the floor and flushed it away with water. Satisfied he had covered up his crime, he drove home to get some sleep.

His guilt kept him away from the warehouse for a few weeks, but in the end, greed got the best of him. He drove down again and grabbed two boxes to take them home. They were full of papers and photos. The papers described how his father had hired a company to find the time machine and pull it up. It also described all of his failed efforts in trying to restore the thing. There was no one who could do it, he had concluded.

Mel could again feel millions of dollars slipping away from him. He had murdered to keep the machine, but now it was worthless. He locked up the warehouse one last time and walked away.

Bryan had not come back. Mary called the police. They couldn't find him. After a couple of weeks, they found his car. It had been stolen, and parked down by the waterfront. There was no blood in it. It wasn't the crime scene.

Chapter Six

New York City
1948

Mel sat at home, the doors locked and the curtain drawn. *I killed a man.* The scene played back time after time in his mind. *I can go to the police and turn myself in for manslaughter.* He shook his head. *No. No one knows what I did. They'll never find me.* Opening up the boxes he brought home from the warehouse, he went through them again. It took his mind off of his problems. *I can go back in time and stop the murder if I can figure this out. Murder? I'm a murderer!* He shook involuntarily.

As he read, he felt his father's hopelessness. "I have worked on this twenty-three years and am no closer to figuring out how to repair it than when I brought it up from the depths of the ocean. My only hope is talking to Robert, something I vowed I would never do. He's the only one who knows how it works."

Robert? Who's Robert? He slammed the papers down on the desk. *I'm not only a murderer, I killed a man over a bunch of worthless metal.*

Detective Caswell looked over the car. It wasn't much to go on, but he had found plenty of fingerprints on it. He didn't have anyone to match them up with. Having become unbound, Bryan Dalton's body floated to the surface of New York harbor two days after he was reported missing. It was now a murder investigation. The statement from the family lawyer about Bryan going to reclaim a plane stuck in his head. The docks were in a rough part of town. Bryan could have been mugged, but why would they move the car? He had to talk to that lawyer again.

"How can I help you?" Mr. Walker was all smiles as Detective Caswell entered his office.

"The body of Bryan Dalton washed up on shore this morning. We've not released any information to the newspaper yet, so keep it under your hat for now." The lawyer's mouth gaped open. To Caswell, the man looked really upset. He couldn't figure if it was from losing a client or he really liked Dalton. The detective wasn't big on lawyers.

"That's terrible."

"Now it's a murder investigation. Do you know who Dalton was going to visit?"

"A man named Mel Hart. He's in possession of the plane that Bryan wanted."

"Where's the plane, and where can I find Mr. Hart?"

Walker wrote both addresses down and handed them to the detective.

"Thank you very much."

The guard at the gate had seemed to hesitate to allow the officer in. After a minute, though, the gate opened. The warehouse unit was locked, so Caswell looked around. The area between the door and edge of the dock looked like it had been freshly cleaned. Right at the edge of the dock, there were scrape marks, like something metallic had been dragged over it. The detective looked over the edge. *Aha, blood.* Taking samples, the detective made his way back to the door of the building and dusted it for fingerprints. When he was finished, he walked over to the guard and talked to him.

Mel answered the knock on the door and stood face to face with Detective Caswell with two police officers standing behind him. "Hello?"

"You're under arrest for the murder of Bryan Dalton." Mel was handcuffed and taken to the station. He didn't utter a word the whole way.

At the station he was fingerprinted and put in a holding cell. A few hours later, a police sergeant stood over the detective's desk. "The fingerprints are a match."

"Good, I'll bring in Mr. Hart for questioning. I'm sure he's cooled his heels long enough."

The sergeant smiled.

All the bravado Mel planned on using when questioned had left him hours ago. He was a beaten man by the time they sat him down in the interview room.

The detective walked in and sat down. "Mr. Hart, do you know why you're here?"

"How dare you accuse me of murder? I was home that night."

"What night are you talking about?" The detective smiled.

"Every night. I didn't kill anyone."

"Why were your fingerprints on Bryan Dalton's car?"

Mel swallowed hard. "I don't know who you're talking about."

"You don't have a prayer. I've got your fingerprints at the dock and on the car. I have the guard telling me you drove Dalton's car away from the pier. All I have to do is connect the dots for the jury and you'll fry in the electric chair."

"You don't have a body. You can't convict without a body," Mel blurted out.

Caswell threw the photos of Bryan's body on the table. "Oh, but I do have a body."

Mel buried his head in his hands. "I didn't mean to do it. He was going to take the plane. I thought was worth millions. Come to find out, it isn't worth a dime."

Chapter Seven

New York Waterfront
1949

"So, what is it? Some type of jet plane?" Gerald Mesh asked. The little man had a high-pitched voice.

"I suppose so. It doesn't work, but for some reason it's worth killing for." Henry Sandoval walked around the plane. The tarp that covered it was old and moth-eaten.

"Killing?"

"Two men fought over this plane. One wound up dead. I got it for back rent on the warehouse bay. I've pushed every button it has, but I can't make it go."

"You try putting gas in it?"

"Of course, I did. Premium, the best that money can buy. The oil leaks out the side, so I plugged the holes."

Gerald walked up to the plane to get a closer look. "Duct tape? You plugged the holes with duct tape?"

"It ain't going nowhere. Duct tape will work fine."

Gerald shook his head. They both walked around the plane for a few minutes. "What are you going to do with it?"

"Sell it."

"To who?"

Henry scratched his head. "I haven't gotten that far yet. I'll figure out something. For now, I'm going to leave it right here."

B. B. Griggs, of the Griggs Salvage Company, stood before the plane. He hadn't seen anything like it before. And if he hadn't, nobody else had, because he'd seen it all. The tall man with beady eyes walked slowly around it. *Some top-secret military project that fell into the wrong hands no doubt. They would pay millions to get it back.* He would have rubbed his hands together for joy, but Henry was watching him like a hawk. If he was looking for any facial expression, there wasn't any. "So how much do you want for it?"

"I'm figuring five million."

Griggs would have paid that in a heartbeat, but that's not how the game was played. He shook his head slowly back and forth. "My dear fellow, I don't know what you think you've got, but It's worth only a few thousand. It's all beat up. I'm certain it doesn't work. I'll I can do is break it apart and sell off the pieces."

"But, but." Henry composed himself. "I'm standin' fast at a million. Not a penny less."

Griggs rubbed his chin as he took another walk around the plane. "I'm feeling charitable, I'll give you ten thousand."

Henry deflated. "It's a time machine. You can control the world with it. Five hundred thousand, no less."

"I see. And if you could control the world, then you wouldn't be selling it, would you? The fact is, I'm not the first person you've had here. Politicians, Army officials, Collectors maybe. They've all told you the same thing. It isn't worth that much. What was the highest bid you've gotten for it?"

"Fifty thousand."

It was a lie. Ten thousand was his highest offer. Griggs knew the game and all the players. "Fine, fifty-five thousand and it's a deal."

They shook hands.

Two days later the machine was moved to Griggs Marine Salvage sheds two piers down the waterfront. He had an army of experts go over every inch. A few days later his chief engineer sat across from him at the table.

"We don't know what half of that stuff is, Sir. Some technologies are barely coming online, others, well, we just don't know. You said this plane could be from the future. I laughed inside when you said it, frankly. Now, I'm a believer. We can't fix it."

"It's worse than that. I've had my man in the Pentagon send out feelers to see if there was some secret project that has gone missing. No luck." Griggs leaned back in his chair. "Box it up and hide it in the back corner of the storage. I'll give it twenty years then try again."

"Yes, Sir."

The large wooden box was pushed into place by two forklifts. Stenciled on the side was "Priority Low, 1969" It was Griggs code. His dreams of riches from the plane had faded, like so many others before him. Still, he hadn't given up altogether. Maybe someday it would be worth the millions he hoped for.

Chapter Eight

Washington D.C.
2044

Charles Gilman, professor of history at Johns Hopkins University, looked up as a man entered his office. The appointment had been set the week before. He had all week to try and find out why a United States Senator wanted to visit him, but try as he could, he was still clueless. The grey-haired professor took off his reading glasses. His eyes were a vivid blue, but deep set with wrinkled skin around them. "How may I help you, Senator?"

"I need you to find something for me."

The professor's eyebrows almost touched as he wrinkled his forehead. "Sir?"

Senator James took a seat across from him. "I need to swear you to secrecy."

"That will be easy. I don't know anything."

Adjusting his tie, the senator continued. "A plane didn't make it back after a mission and disappeared. I need you to find it."

"Me? but…"

"You don't understand, I know. This plane disappeared around the turn of the last century."

The professor's stared at him blankly before responding. "Are we talking the year 2000 or the year 1900?"

"1900."

The professor smiled. "That one is easy, there were no planes then."

James leaned forward until he was uncomfortably close. "There was one. A time machine. It is something very out of place for the period. I need it found. Millions of research dollars for your department are on the line."

Gilman leaned back to put some space between the two of them. "I, um, it's hard to believe, is all."

"You don't need to 'believe,' just find it. Also find Robert Dalton, he was the pilot." Not waiting for an answer, James stood up and left.

The professor shook his head. His department relied heavily on the funding they received from the government and James held the purse strings. He would have to do something. Reluctantly, he headed down to the archives.

It was a needle in a haystack, but that was what the professor was good at, finding needles. A murder case he stumbled across was the very first piece of the puzzle. The defendant, Mel Hart mentioned something about a time machine during the sentencing phase of his murder trial. The man he murdered was one Bryan Dalton, son of R. Adalwolf Dalton. Could that be Robert Adalwolf Dalton?

Following up on the lead, he found a court order for Mel Hart to hand over an airplane to Bryan Dalton. There was no indication that it ever happened. A plane was sold from that location by the owner of the dock. The trail stopped at Griggs Salvage Company. Two reasons for a trail stopping in Gilman's experience, it was the end of the trail, or worse, the records were lost.

With thoughts of his grant money disappearing, he headed over to Robison Recycling, the ones who bought out Griggs, to see what records they had.

Standing up from his desk, a tall Ralf Robison asked. "Professor Gilman, how can I help you?"

"I'm looking for something that is lost to history. It was traced to the Grigg's Salvage. It's an airplane that was purchased in 1949."

"Oh, the heap, that's what we call it. Old man Griggs wouldn't let us scrap it for the metal, my father vowed he wouldn't when he bought the company, now that I own it, I've kept it crated up according to his wishes. As soon as he's gone, though, so is the heap."

The professor rushed back to his office and called James. "I found your time machine." Gilman smiled. He was getting his grant money after all.

It took a while for Senator James to make it to the office. By then, Gilman was having second thoughts. When James strolled in, Gilman confronted him. "It's an insane thing you are doing. Changing the timeline could destroy our very existence. I beg of you, leave well enough alone."

"You'll get your grant money. That's all you scholarly type want, isn't it? Look how much more research you will be able to do when the timeline changes. Besides, we've already gone back in time and we're still here."

Reluctantly, the professor gave him the location. A few million dollars later, the Vmax3 drive, along with what was left of the airframe, was headed on a train to Seattle.

Atlantic Ocean

The boat chugged up and back, with three fishing lines in the water. There were no hooks, just weights to make it look like they were on a fishing charter. There was a large cable with an electrical line out the back of the ship, for the side scanning radar. Other than that, the disguise was perfect.

A captain and three crew members were on the boat. Two of the men were in the cabin, monitoring the images of the seafloor. The other was watching to make sure the cables weren't getting tangled. The captain spent most of his time in the flying bridge, steering the ship, but came down once in a while to check the status of the operation.

They'd been doing this for four days now. They had covered all the places that the plane should have come down. Dempsey brought out his laptop again. He was losing faith in his estimates. He had gone over and over the model. The plane had to be here. Right here.

Instead of looking at the monitor, General Williams scanned the horizon with binoculars. "You know what occurs to me?" he asked Dempsey.

"No, Sir."

"We're not being watched."

"Sir?"

"There's no plane in the sky, no ship from miles around. No drone keeping track of us. Nothing. Senator James would have been spying on at least one of us."

"What would that mean?" Dempsey asked.

"That would mean, Senator James already has the plane. We're wasting our time."

"But sir, he'll destroy time."

Williams set down the binoculars. "I'm afraid you're right."

Chapter Nine

Seattle, Washington
2044

Phillip Anderson smiled. "Lockheed is laying off, so to get them to take on a new project was enticing. We have all the men who built the original Vmax3 drive. With their memories and our copy of it, it should be a breeze to reconstruct."

Phillip shouldn't have been there. He, like Senator James, didn't have a security clearance. James was writing the checks, however, so what he said went. It didn't matter that Anderson had been convicted of espionage and sentenced to life in prison. A presidential pardon, in exchange for James finding funding for a special project, freed Anderson.

Phillip would be the pilot. His first mission, go get Dalton and bring him back. James felt a need to yell and scream at him for the failure in killing Hitler. Then he would send Dalton and Anderson back to try and get rid of Hitler again.

The airframe had been beyond repair because of all the corrosion. This was a huge setback. Even James, who was an expert in shifting money around, couldn't shift this much without getting the attention of a committee somewhere. It didn't matter. With a time machine, he could get rid of his political adversaries in the past, before they became a problem. A few investments in the right securities would help recoup the money, too. All he had to do was stall until the machine was operational.

He would deal with that later. For now he smiled. "Excellent."

Work went a lot slower than he anticipated. A CIA agent was poking around. Special Agent Carlson began looking into the missing money. The man had close-cropped hair and looked like a bulldog to James. His nose was a stub and crunched. He followed a scent like a bulldog. James couldn't shake the man.

The man had interviewed James three times already. He didn't seem to like the answers, because another interview was scheduled.

James stroked his chin as he thought about it. *CIA, agent indeed. There's nothing special about him. I'll wipe him from the history books, just after I get rid of Hitler.*

Phillip burst into the office where the Senator had set up shop. "The Vmax3 drive is done. It's on a truck and headed this way."

If James could have danced, he would have. "Ahead of schedule!"

"There's a problem, though." Phillip wasn't smiling. "The men down there say that they are being talked to by Carlson. One by one. If one of them knows too much and slips, we're done for."

"I'll tell Boeing we need that airframe sooner. They're used to working massive overtime. They can start doing it on my plane."

"Yes, Sir. I'll let them know the schedule just got moved up."

A month later, the engine was mated to the fuselage. James had moved back to Washington DC to distract the investigators. He would do no tests this time. The plane would take off in the middle of the night and bring Dalton back. With the day set, the senator relaxed.

When he arrived at his office the next morning, three CIA agents were waiting for him. Carlson handed him a piece of paper. "Senator, we are taking over your project. You will no longer have any contact with anyone involved with it."

The senator checked his watch. "You're too late. The plane has already taken off. By the time Phillip Anderson has completed his missions, Mr. Carlson, you will no longer exist. You will die of SIDS at the age of one. In fact, I expect you to disappear any second now."

"That's it, I'm arresting you for murder." Carlson pushed the senator against the wall and handcuffed him.

"You're going to have a very hard time proving murder if it happens in the past. Your friends here will never know you existed. Your investigation will have never have happened. I can't have murdered you, you're still alive."

It was the first time the agents seem to understand what they were dealing with. Each looked at the other searching for answers, but none of them had any. Carlson undid the cuffs and left. He knew he couldn't charge the man with his murder if he was still alive.

James rubbed his wrists. He had made up the whole story. Phillip was going back in time to get Dalton, which was the only mission currently. It would be two days before he left.

Chapter Ten

The Hamptons, New York
1912

Adalwolf Dalton was shaken awake by his wife. "What is that sound?"

No sooner had she asked than a light from the outside of the house illuminated the bedroom.

Dalton stood up, put on his pants and grabbed his pistol from the drawer. "It's bad news. It's the time machine."

He headed outside his home to the back yard. The plane had landed and the pilot was getting out. When he looked over at Dalton, he held up his hands. "Whoa, buddy, I'm here to rescue you."

"I don't want to be rescued." He concentrated on the man's face. "Phillip Anderson, is that you?"

"In the flesh. Can you put down the gun?"

Dalton pointed the gun at the ground. "I thought you were in prison."

"Presidential pardon arraigned by my friend, Senator James. I'm here to find out what went wrong and to fix it. Senator James still wants Hitler dead."

"It doesn't work. Without Hitler, the communists come to power. The United States is attacked on all sides. The timeline is a nightmare. No, Hitler must stay alive."

"What about stopping the holocaust?"

Dalton shook his head. "Far worse things happen to the Jews under the communists."

"I don't believe that. Listen, come back with me and you can explain everything to them."

Dalton felt Mary come up behind him. He swallowed hard. Senator James had the time machine, he had to stop him, one way or another. "No, this ends here. I can't let you go back." He pointed the gun at Phillip.

Phillip's eyes widened. "You can't be serious." He held up his hands again.

Dalton's eight-year-old son, Bryan, wrapped his arms around Dalton's leg. "What's happening, Daddy? I'm scared."

"This is a bad man."

Phillip smiled, he seemed to know Dalton couldn't kill him with his wife and kid watching. "I guess I'll be on my way, good buddy."

"Before you go, how did you get the Vmax drive?"

"A New York stockbroker found it. No, he knew you somehow and he traced it back. Found the ship's log that picked you up. He traced the location from there. It took him years. He pulled it up in 1925. He had no idea how to fix it, so it sat in a warehouse until we found it. The airframe was trash, so we had to construct a new one. No problem for Senator James. It was the Vmax 3 drive we needed. The original plans were destroyed. It was beyond repair, but all the components were there. We reverse engineered it."

"You should destroy it, before it destroys you. I was lucky to fix the timeline."

"Not to worry, I'll go back in time and rescue you out of the ocean. I'll bet you'll be more willing to go with me then. See you in a few minutes." Phillip climbed in the plane.

Dalton was having none of it. He walked over to the side of the plane and shot the oil tank. He emptied his clip on it. Phillips hurried to start the engine and fly away.

Eight-year-old Bryan was screaming and his wife ran up to him. "Did you kill him?"

Dalton hugged his son. "The bad man isn't hurt." He picked up his son and faced his wife. "He isn't hurt, but he won't make it back to his time. The fatal flaw with his machine is the position of the oil tank. They didn't fix that when they built the new one. The drive that lets time travel happen won't work for very long."

"Is he going to be stuck in the past like you are?"

"Yes," he smiled and kissed her. "It isn't so bad."

"I'm glad you didn't go with him. I wondered all these years, if you would, if given a chance. Now I know."

They walked back into the house. "Yes, I do love you, although I miss my Ipad."

"Your what?"

"It's a, ah well. It's hard to explain is what it is." Dalton put the gun in his pocket. He hoped he did enough damage to the machine to stop it. Phillip Anderson wouldn't care about timelines and people's lives. He would do whatever Senator James told him, no matter who it affected. His heart racing, Dalton lay back down, his wife and eight-year-old in the bed. The boy had stopped crying at least. Dalton knew he wouldn't be able to sleep.

The next morning, Dalton sat at his desk. He needed to find the airplane and destroy it. It was a nightmare that they had built another one. *They can replace it over and over again.* He shivered. He had to do something. He knew it was up to him. Ross and Williams were probably unaware any of this was going on.

If Anderson was able to fix the plane, he could go back farther in time. *Would I go with him?* He didn't like Anderson, but getting plucked out of the ocean or off that freighter might have a way to convince him to go back to his own time.

How much damage would they do to the timeline? His very existence was threatened.

He felt his wife's gentle hand on his shoulder. "It will be fine, sweetheart."

I could lose everything I have and I wouldn't even know it. He sighed. He stood up and hugged her.

"The time machine was amazing. If I had any lingering doubts about your crazy story, they all disappeared last night."

"They should not have built another one. They should have let the whole idea go." He kept holding her.

"What will they do now?"

"That machine won't make it back to its own time. I shot low enough to ensure that all the oil will leak out. I don't know how they found me. It's very upsetting. They will have to build another. Of course, it could show up tomorrow with another pilot. Once they use this time and date, there is nothing stopping them from doing it again."

"They could show up tomorrow, even though it will take them years to build another one?" Her wide eyes gazed intently into his.

"They could show up tomorrow, or yesterday. It's not good for us."

"You need to go out and get more bullets," she insisted.

"I'm getting a bigger gun while I'm at it. Next time they might fix that fatal flaw."

They busied themselves around the house, trying to forget what had happened. It was a deep feeling of helplessness to think that another time machine could land without warning.

Dalton checked his correspondence. The stocks were paying off. His steel mill was churning out raw material for cannons and guns. It was making him rich. It also gave him an underlying guilt. He would be providing the means for the great destruction that would happen in two short years.

When Mary came in, Dalton turned to her. "We need to get David back home. Europe's not going to be a safe place soon. Your brother has done a tremendous work there, though.

"I'll send him a telegram to come back. I have missed him so."

"Tell him not to come through England. Leave from a German port instead."

"Any particular reason?" She stared at him intently.

His knowledge of the future upset her often. This was one of those times. How could he tell her over a thousand people would soon die in the middle of the Atlantic Ocean? "It will be safer."

She shook her head. "I'll tell him it's important. I do wish you could confide in me. I would like to know what's going on."

"It's going to be bad, that's all I can tell you. He needs to leave through Germany."

She nodded and walked away.

Chapter Eleven

The Hamptons, New York
1912

The eight-year-old, Bryan, was having nightmares again. "Bad man from the sky is at our house," He screamed.

Dalton woke and sat bolt upright in be, then reached for his gun. Mary gently touched his hand. "Honey, it's another nightmare is all."

He took a deep breath. Peeking out the window to make sure, he rolled over and laid back down.

Mary went in to comfort their son. Fifteen minutes later, she came back to bed. "He's asleep. I don't know how long he'll stay that way. The time machine really upset him. It's upset you too I see."

"Haven't had a good night's sleep since it landed. I had hoped it was over."

"Are we going to have this hanging over our heads for the rest of our lives?"

"I'm afraid so."

She put her arm around him. "You didn't go back with them. I guess I'm more important than an Ipad."

He laughed. It eased his tension.

In the morning, a currier brought in a large crate. Dalton smiled as he wheeled it in the house. Mary's forehead creased. "What is that, dear?"

"I pulled in a favor from one of my companies. It's a bigger gun. I will stop them after all."

She shook her head. "Boys and their toys."

He sat the box down and busied himself at his desk. The door chimed again, this time Mary went to answer it. She came back into the room. "Honey, you said for David not to come back through England, but he couldn't get across the channel, so he had to."

Dalton snapped his head around. "What port, what ship?"

She stepped back in surprise. "Um, it doesn't say what ship, but the telegram was sent from Southampton."

"Oh, no." He stood up and stared out the window. "No!"

"What is it?" Mary grabbed Dalton's arm to turn him around. "What is it?"

His voice was muted. "The Titanic leaves from Southampton. It's going to sink."

"We have to stop it! Send a telegram. Tell them to change course, tell them to return to port."

He hung his head. "I can't. I changed history by letting one little boy die. If I let a thousand live, no timeline will be safe. No, the *Titanic* must sink. They will pass new laws. Ocean travel will be safer."

"But, David? Will he die? How can you just stand there when his life is in peril?"

"I can't do anything. I won't do anything. I told him what not to do. He did it anyway." He kicked the wall.

"Well, I can do something." She stormed out of the house.

He sat down heavily in his chair. His world had just come crashing down. She knew now he wouldn't stop history, for David or for her. He thought about going after her, but decided to let her go.

An hour later, she came back. Running in, she hugged him. "He isn't on the Titanic. Another telegram from him arrived while I was at their office."

She read the telegram. "Uncle Adalwolf, I hope you're not mad at me. I tried to get on the Titanic, but she had sailed. Will be taking the SS. New York City, but there is a coal strike here, so she is delayed."

He held up the telegram and said to it, "No, David, I'm not mad at you."

Mary stepped back. "You would've let him die."

"I already impacting everything, by just being here. I want to minimize that contact."

"When are all those people going to die?"

"In a day or two. I don't remember the exact day, but soon."

"Is there nothing we can do? A thousand people? How horrible." Tears streaked her face.

Dalton put his arm around her. "It's the past where I came from. It was still a very sad thing, but just the beginning of sad things. Worse tragedies than that are on the horizon. It's best that we don't discuss them ahead of time. It all has to turn out this way or we are the reason for the suffering we create by changing the timeline."

Mary was quiet for the rest of the evening.

A few weeks later, when the SS New York City arrived in New York, both Adalwolf and Mary were there to greet David.

"I couldn't find passage in France or Germany, Uncle. I'm sorry, but I had to leave from England. I hope you're not angry at me."

Dalton ruffled his hair. "It's so great to have you back in one piece."

Mary hugged David. "Welcome home."

Chapter Twelve

Issaquah, Washington
1970

Phillip had heard the thuds against the fuselage as Dalton shot his plane. *He's crazy.* Wasting no time in getting airborne, Phillips had flown away quickly. Not knowing how badly the plane was damaged, he decided not to go further back in time, but go forward, to his own time, to have the plane repaired.

When he was high in the sky, he switched on the Vmax 3 drive, setting it for the year 2032. It came to life the plane buffeted wildly. This was normal. What wasn't normal was the engine smoke billowing out the back. Soon the drive stopped working

His heart racing, Phillip tried to switch it on again, but it didn't work. *Where am I? When am I?*

The warning lights in the flight deck flashed on and off. and alarms blared, forcing him to shut down the Vmax3 drive. He flew on to the Seattle area, landing in the clearing of a forest.

Forget it, I'm not going back to rescue that lunatic, he seethed. He climbed out of the plane to check the damage. Seeing all the oil in the tank was gone, he knew right away he was stuck in the past. "Dalton," he screamed, shaking his fist in the air.

It had been Senator James' idea to go get Dalton. James put his best man into finding Dalton. It took a long time to locate him. There were several places in history where they knew where he was. The surest place was the house in the Hamptons. That is where they decided to go. It had all been a big mistake. They hadn't calculated on Dalton wanting to stay with his wife and family.

Making his way out of the woods, Phillip found a road to follow. It wasn't long before a car happened by. He thumbed it down, but instead of giving him a ride, the driver waited until he was close to yell, "Get a job, you hippie."

The tires squealed as the man drove off.

1970's Impala. Phillip sighed. He hoped it was a restored car, but he suspected it wasn't. He sat down by a tree and watched five more cars pass by. All the cars were late sixties models or early seventies. *Not good, not good at all. I can't get the replacement parts in this time period. Forget saving Dalton, I'm going to kill him.*

He had no means of transportation, except a plane that was low on fuel. His rage got the best of him and he screamed again. "Dalton!" *I'll get my revenge.* He didn't know how or where, but he would do it.

The money he had brought with him was a mix of 1900 and 2034 bills, none of which would work in 1970. He went back to the plane, grabbed the gun, put the camouflage over the plane, and made his way into town.

Deciding the easiest way to get some money was to stick up a convenience store, he strode in wearing pants and a t-shirt. Pointing the gun at the attendant, he demanded cash. What he didn't see was the shotgun poking out from behind the office door. A loud blast, and Phillip fell to the ground. As he lay there bleeding, he swore again. "I'll get that Dalton." It was the last thing he said.

The detective assigned to the case, Greg Watson, had the dead man's pocket contents brought to his desk. It was a strange mixture of IDs and strange money.

"What do you make of it, Bill?" he asked a fellow detective.

"What you have is a Sci-Fi man. Thinks he can travel back and forth between centuries."

Greg laughed. "I suppose you're right. Too many *Twilight Zone* episodes. My guess is that all these are fakes. He's going to be another John Doe. I'll let the county figure out what they want to do with the body."

The city ran his picture in the paper asking anybody that might know the name of the man to come forward. No one ever did. In an unmarked grave on the edge of the cemetery, Phillip Anderson's body was laid to rest. No funeral or eulogy, just John Doe 23 on the headstone.

Chapter Thirteen

Issaquah, Washington
1971

Doug Tatum and his son Carl were deer hunting in the foothills of the Cascades when they came across a clearing.

"Dad, there's something strange here."

Both men looked at the camouflage netting. It was faded, and they could see a metallic object in the middle of it. Doug pulled back the fabric and looked underneath. "It's a plane."

"No way. How could they get a plane out here? There isn't an airfield."

"Look for yourself then."

Carl peeked under the cover. "Let's pull this off."

Both men tugged on the netting. There was no doubt as to what the object was. "We need to call the air force," Doug said.

"Why. They won't give us a reward. I think we try to sell it to a collector of some sort."

"No, I don't want to steal government property. I'll have to look over my shoulder for the rest of my life. Let's tell the government where they can find their plane. Then we forget we were ever here."

Carl heaved a sigh.

Back on the main road, they stopped in at a truck stop and called McChord Air Force Base. The next morning the two men waited for the olive drab car to pull over. An army lieutenant hopped out. "You must be the men that found the missing air force property."

"Yes, I'm Doug Tatum and this is my son Carl."

"Glad to meet you. Can you lead me to it?"

It was an hour before they finished the trek back to the airplane. The officer's jaw dropped. "I've never seen anything like this before."

"I thought you guys were searching for it," Carl said.

"Nope."

He shook his head. "You mean, I could have sold it to a collector?"

The next morning, a platoon of airmen arrived at the site, along with a two-star general. An investigative team took pictures from all directions. It was unlike anything they had seen.

"How did this thing get in here?" the general asked.

The lieutenant pointed to the fan blades on the wing. "It looks like it landed here, Sir. The engine has ducting that goes to the wings. It's a vertical takeoff and landing airplane, like a helicopter."

"The U. S. is still experimenting with that. We haven't perfected it yet."

"Someone did, Sir."

The general shook his head. "Those top-secret types never tell us anything. How do we get this thing out of here?"

"The army has some Chinooks at Ft. Lewis," the lieutenant replied.

"Get them on the horn."

Two days later, the plane was sitting in a hangar at McChord field. It was covered with tarps and guarded by two dozen MPs. Two CIA agents and the general in charge of military intelligence drove up to it. The hanger doors were closed before the tarps were taken off. "This isn't one of ours, the general said."

The base commandant looked at him. "Who's is it, then?"

"I have no idea."

The commandant cracked his knuckles. "Let's put some gas in it and see what this sucker can do."

"Sounds like an idea. I want the mechanics to look at it first, though."

Several airmen worked on the machine for the next two weeks. They went all over it, trying to figure out the controls. When the commandant and the general returned, the mechanical report was in.

"The plane has two engines. One that powers the airframe and no one knows what the other one does. The top engine was frozen beyond repair. All of the components were foreign to the mechanics. No way to fix the top engine. The bottom engine, however, was serviceable. Each engine had its own oil tank. The top engine's oil tank was shot full of holes."

A pilot familiarized himself with the controls while the mechanics were working on it. He was ready to go.

The plane was wheeled out to the tarmac. The pilot climbed in and turned it on. He was able to take off and land several times. He even took it up vertically and hovered before bringing it back down vertically.

They adjourned to a conference room after the demonstration. "That's an amazing machine," the commandant said. "I wonder if it can be duplicated."

The lead mechanic piped up. "No, Sir. We don't even know what some of these parts are. There is no way we can replicate them. The most disturbing thing is the manufacturing dates on all of the components have been blanked out. Someone is trying to cover up something. The rear seat has controls for changing dates. It's like it can travel through time or something. It was set for July 17, 2032."

"We'll send it to Special Operations, see what they can make of it," the general said.

"Yes, Sir," the commandant replied.

The general added, "If anyone comes around asking about this plane, I want them investigated."

Chapter Fourteen

Washington DC
2044

Senator James walked into the office of Professor Gilman. He didn't wait for the professor to say anything, but burst out, "My plane didn't return. I need you to find it again."

"That's not a bad thing. If you succeed in your missions, then my forty-two years of knowledge will be useless. What's the point, anyway? We've survived in this timeline. Why don't you leave well enough alone?"

The senator stomped his foot. "We've discussed this already. I want my ship back." Taking a deep breath, the senator continued. "Please try and find out where it is."

"Why don't you just build another one?"

"I can't afford to. Already, the House is looking into my finances. They are talking about an investigation."

"I see. Yes, of course. I'll try and find your ship. I wonder if Major Dalton was in it when it disappeared, or if he's stuck in yet another timeline. The poor man. I was so hoping you could bring him back. If he wants to come, that is."

"Why wouldn't he want to come back? Who would want to be stuck in the past?"

"Yes, you're probably right. That will help in my search."

James made his way back to his office. His personal secretary had left him a note on his computer keyboard. It was after hours and she had gone home.

Representative Davis was in again. He wants some financial records and was very upset you weren't here. He says he'll be back first thing in the morning.

James wadded up the note and threw it away. If there was anything he hated, it was someone demanding something from him. He wasn't going to cooperate. He had spent too much on the time machine and now his enemies were gathering like a pack of wolves that smelled blood.

Professor Gilman began his research. He worked best late at night. He hated Senator James, but then again, everyone hated Senator James, so he was in the majority. It was a needle in a haystack. Almost impossible to find. His discovery of Dalton had been hard enough. Dalton wanted to be found for some reason, but even then, it was difficult.

After working for several hours, he made an interesting discovery. Dalton hadn't moved. He spent the rest of his life in the Hamptons. Gilman scratched his chin. The plane might not have reached him. The professor then started on the children. The oldest, Bryan, lived in the house after his father died. He once commented about having nightmares. He told of a plane landing in his yard when he was a child. That caught Gilman's attention. *A child?* Born in 1904, there wouldn't be many planes around when he was a child.

Browsing through the records, there was no newspaper article of a crash in the Hamptons, or even a plane there. It had to be Senator James' time machine. *Why didn't Dalton go back with him? Of course, he didn't want to leave his family. He had adapted by then.*

Did Dalton destroy the machine? That was a question the professor couldn't answer.

All of his classes were canceled the next day as he went through every record he could find. He called Senator James up with the bad news. "There is no sign of your plane in history. I don't have access to a lot of the government records going back to the 1960s. Even though it's over the twenty-five-year period that they are to be reviewed, they are still secret. Can you get me access to those?"

"I'll see what I can do."

Senator James paid the Secretary of Defense a visit. He was a large man, broad across the shoulders and had a husky voice. "What do you want, James?" He folded his arms, waiting for a reply.

"I need some historical records from the seventies that are still classified for some unexplained reason."

The Secretary shook his head. "They will remain classified."

Senator James' voice went up several octaves. "Why? I need them."

"I know why, and they will remain classified."

James stormed out of the office.

The Secretary pulled his phone out. "We have someone asking about the X32 file. Senator James."

"I see. We'll deal with this right away."

Chapter Fifteen

Washington DC
2044

When James arrived back at his office, his secretary's cheeks had a red flush to them. She only did this when she was upset. "Sir, you have a subpoena to appear before the House committee investigating the missing funds."

The senator's shoulders sagged. He didn't have time to say anything as four men entered his office. "Senator James, FBI. We need you to come with us."

"I will not."

Two of the men grabbed his arms and cuffed him.

"This is an outrage." He screamed as he was taken away.

His secretary snapped up the phone and started making calls.

In the back seat, between two agents, James was still complaining.

"Sir, you have the right to remain silent. I suggest you use it," one of the men said.

The car parked in front of a large building. James was pulled out and then uncuffed. One of the men held the door open and the five of them entered. There before them was the plane with the Vmax3 drive.

"You found it. This is Air Force property. I demand you return it to me at once."

"You're in no position to demand anything, Senator. You will tell us what this thing does and how we fix it."

James turned to see the Secretary of Defense, Trevor Osterman, standing behind him. "I will do nothing of the sort."

"You're in enough trouble, Senator. We can add to that if you don't cooperate."

James walked around the machine. Ignoring the secretary, he asked, "Where's the Vmax3 drive?"

Osterman motioned with his head, and two men wheeled the badly damaged engine from around the corner. "Is this the Vmax3 drive?"

"Yes, that's it. What happened to it?"

"From what we can see, the oil tank was shot and the engine seized up."

"Dalton. He did this. He didn't want to come back. Where's Phillip Anderson?"

"You have a story to tell us, Senator. I don't know anything about a Phillip Anderson. This plane was found in 1971, near Issaquah, Washington."

"1971? He didn't make it back. I need to fix up that drive right away. I have to rescue him."

"First off, Senator, all of your accounts have been frozen. Second off, are you talking about going into the past? Is this a time machine?"

The senator turned pale. He had talked too much again. "I can't say anything more."

"Come on, Senator. You've already given up the chicken coop. You're about to go down on charges of misappropriation of government funds. I can make all that go away. What is this thing and how do we fix it?"

"If I tell you what it is, I want complete control of it." The senator folded his arms.

"No, you get nothing but the inside of a prison cell. This plane has been sitting here sixty-one years, a few more won't matter. We'll figure it out eventually. Take him away."

"Wait," the senator pleaded. "I have plans for the Vmax3 engine. I can fix it."

Osterman motioned to his men. "Take the senator to wherever he has the plans and bring them back here."

'Yes, Sir."

"You don't understand. The plans are in Seattle."

"I don't care where they are. You need to get them here as soon as possible."

The senator swallowed. He knew he would never give the plans over. These people would destroy the timeline with their careless use of the plane. All he wanted was to get out of this situation. He would then try to get the plane back. He couldn't afford to build another. "Colonel Ross has them. He was in charge of the development team. Project Blackhole. Look it up. Those are the men you want. They have the plans."

"You'd better be telling me the truth or I'll make sure your cellmate is the biggest, meanest man in the prison," Osterman said.

"I am telling the truth. Project Blackhole." The senator was getting his confidence back. Those men wouldn't tell Osterman anything. He knew the secret was safe with them. While the FBI was terrorizing them, the senator would testify in front of Congress, and the whole nation, that there was a secret weapon the FBI had and the Air Force needed it back. The mission would change. He would go back in time and kill Osterman in the hospital, while he was still a baby.

Chapter Sixteen

The Hamptons, New York
2044

General Williams was very surprised to see two FBI agents standing on his front porch. "What do you want?"

"You're wanted for questioning."

"For what?" the general demanded.

"We can't discuss that here."

"I'm not going anywhere without my lawyer."

The agents didn't know what to do. One turned back and called his boss. A minute later, he faced Williams again. "You can call your lawyer on the way."

"Am I under arrest?" the general asked.

"No, Sir."

"Then get off my property."

Defeated, the agents left. It wasn't a minute later that his phone rang. It was Colonel Ross. "General, were you just visited by some goons?"

"Yes, you too, I take it."

"Yes. I sent them packing. I think they'll come back though. One of them mentioned Project Blackhole and Senator James."

The general sighed. "With the investigation into his shady dealings, I wondered how long it would take him to crack." Williams knew he shouldn't say more as their phones were more than likely tapped, but he added, "At least we've destroyed the plans for the Vmax3 drive so no one will ever use it again."

Ross must have realized what the general was doing. "Yes, so no one will ever use that terrible machine again. It could have destroyed all our lives. We were lucky last time. We don't want to chance it one more time."

The next day, appointments were made. Colonel Ross, General Williams, and Captain Dempsey, along with their lawyers, stood in front of the time machine at the FBI storage facility.

Secretary Osterman strode in the room like he was on a parade ground. "Gentlemen, you already know what this is. What I need from you is the plans for the Vmax3 drive."

No one answered. The three Air Force men walked around the plane.

Ross whispered to the two others. "There's no corrosion to the aluminum skin. Being in salt water for years should have destroyed it."

Dempsey whispered back, "How did they repair it? They didn't have the Vmax3 drive schematic. We deleted it."

Williams touched the holes in the fuselage. "It's been shot. Someone knew the plane's weak spot. You don't suppose they took it back to get Dalton, do you?"

"Enough of the whispers," Osterman bellowed. "When can I get the plans for the drive?"

Williams faced him. "You can't. They've been destroyed. This plane was used to kill Hitler and stop the Holocaust. It caused a catastrophe to the timeline. The Russians joined the Germans in making almost the entire world communists. Billions die and wars continued. They went back in time and saved Hitler to restore the timeline."

Osterman smiled. "So, it is a time machine. I couldn't get that information out of Senator James. Think of how easily we could destroy enemies of the United States."

"You haven't heard a single word I've said, have you?" Williams asked.

"This is too important not to use. I will need those drawings." Osterman folded his arms.

"You're out of luck. Those have been destroyed," Williams repeated.

"Impossible. How was a second plane built if the drawings were destroyed?"

"A second plane?" Williams' face paled.

"Yes," Osterman replied. "Project Blackhole ended in 2029, this plane was built in 2031. It's a different plane."

Williams glanced over at Ross and Myers. He could tell by the look on their faces, they had no idea it was a new plane. "Senator James is the man you need to talk to. If this is a new plane, he built it. He had all the plans and it's identical to the first one in every way. How he rebuilt the Vmax3 drive, I have no idea. The first plane crashed into the middle of the Atlantic Ocean."

"Go get James," Osterman yelled. His men headed out.

Williams and the rest of them turned to go.

"Don't leave town," Osterman said after them. They didn't bother looking back.

When they were outside, Williams shuddered, "He built another one. We have to destroy that plane before they get James to get them the plans."

"We can't get into the place," Dempsey said as they walked out of the gate.

"We have to try," Williams replied.

Chapter Seventeen

Washington DC
2044

Senator James sat in front of the members of the House of Representatives, plotting which ones he would get rid of when he reacquired his time machine. The hearing had lasted hours and it didn't look like it was going to end anytime soon. Representative Edwards kept harping about the missing five billion dollars. James kept telling them it was for a top-secret project he couldn't discuss.

"Who gave you the authorization to bankroll these projects using federal money?" Edwards glared down at him.

James smiled, despite the grilling. His first mission would be to take out Edwards. History would be some much better off without the man.

"Senator, please answer the question."

"That is top secret also." It wasn't. He'd been able to bankroll the project on his own using funds meant for other projects. He always overfunded the projects from his state to pad his research funds.

"Are we sure you aren't skimming a little money for your own endeavors?"

Yes, I am and that endeavor will eliminate you from the history books. "Why, no, Representative Edwards, I'm not. You've gone over my personal finances with a fine-tooth comb. You haven't found one penny of federal money that I've kept for myself." *Except for the Cayman bank account.* He smiled again at the thought.

Edwards threw his pencil in the air then leaned back in his chair. "This is going nowhere. I'm calling a recess."

The committee split up and headed out. James went straight to his office, checking his computer right away. An angry video message from Williams was all there was. He called him back. "General, let's meet somewhere. I have the information you want and you have the information I want."

Dempsy, Williams, and Ross sat at the café table when James arrived. It was a secluded corner where no one could overhear the conversation. James was with Professor Gilman. He pulled up a chair from another table and the five of them stared at each other for a minute waiting for the first to talk.

James, never one for silence, began. "Gentlemen, this is Professor Gilman. He's an historian, much like Colonel Ross here. He's the one that found the plane."

With all eyes on him, Gilman fidgeted before beginning, "Adalwolf Dalton crashed his plane off the coast, as you know. What you might not have known, is the plane was recoverable. Ted, Adalwolf's old boss, went down and got it. Of course, they couldn't do anything with it. It was stored in a warehouse at the dock for many years. How I found out about it was the lawsuit. Bryan Dalton vs. Mel Hart. The argument was over the ownership of an airplane. Bryan claimed it was his father's and was granted ownership of it. When he went to pick it up, Mel Hart killed him. Mel went down for murder and the airplane went from owner to owner. No one had the technology to fix it. It ended up in a warehouse on the outskirts of Philly."

James smiled, "That's where I came in. I purchased it for a cool million." He cracked his knuckles. "It wasn't fixable, but I sent the fuselage to Boeing and the engine to Lockheed. The men had worked on the originals and with the technologies in front of them, were able to recreate the airplane." He sat back in his chair.

Gilman cleared his throat. "Plane two was sent back to collect Adalwolf. I figure he didn't want to return, so he shot up the oil tank. The plane didn't make it back. It was stuck in the seventies. Two hunters found it in the woods and called in the Air Force."

"Now, gentlemen," The senator folded his arms. "I've told you what I know. I want to hear your side of the story. How did the mission fail and when I get my plane back, how can I make sure it succeeds?"

Williams leaned forward to emphasize his point. "The mission was a success. Hitler drowned. Then the communists took over. They overran Europe and then threatened the United States. Billions died and the Jews were no better off with the communists than with the Germans. Your noble gesture turns out to be a nightmare. Dalton, on figuring this out, went back in time and fixed it. Your time machine will kill us all."

James' shoulders sagged. His eyes were so wide open one would have thought he was going downhill on a rollercoaster that had just derailed.

Gilman scratched his head. "You mean to say, the timeline changed and we knew nothing about it?"

Williams turned to him. "Yes, different timeline, different lives. We will never know. We only live in the here and now. If the timeline changes, our lives are altered, but we never know. Only the two in the plane see the difference." He turned back to Williams. "We need to destroy that plane."

James' eyes were still wide open and beads of sweat dotted his forehead. "They're building another one."

"What!" Williams screamed. The other patrons of the restaurant turned to see what the commotion was.

James waited until they turned back around. "It's out of my control. The CIA got wind of it. They are building the third plane. It's them who are having me investigated. They want to lock me away. My only chance is to get the second plane and go back in time to stop them. They took my men and plans away from me."

Chapter Eighteen

Washington DC
2045

FBI agents were all over the secret compound. It was like an ant hill. Two men sat on the hill waiting for things to calm down. It was a crude but effective plan. The plane would be destroyed. It had to be.

As darkness neared, the number of men working on the Vmax3 drive was reduced. "Time to strike." The camouflaged man nodded. He laid his rifle across the top of the hill. He donned his night scope, after acquiring the target, he slowly squeezed the trigger.

The thought of murdering a fellow American didn't cross his mind. Everything would be undone when they went back in time. For now, he would die. The guard at the gate slumped to the ground. A truck came rushing in, smashed through the gate and through the warehouse door. The driver stopped the truck right by the Vmax3 drive reassembly area, and then pressed the button.

A flash engulfed the building and a raging fire ensued. The driver died instantly. He, too, would live again, per the plan.

Colonel Ross, USAF retired, walked up to the gate and flashed his ID. The guard nodded and buzzed him in. Walking down the long colorless hall, he showed his ID four more times before he was able to enter the caged off room with a single table.

A few minutes later, Senator James, in an orange jumpsuit, was escorted in by two guards. They sat the ex-senator down and walked out.

"I do have to admit, you're easy to find these days." He didn't know why he had come. Maybe to gloat at an old adversary, or maybe he felt sorry for the man. He couldn't decide, but hoped it was the latter.

"I'm hoping you have news that can get me out of here. Did you get control of the…" He stopped to look around to make sure the guards were out of earshot. "Well, you know what."

"I have news. The FBI's version of the 'machine' was destroyed. It was reported as a terrorist attack. The airframe and the engine were both blown to smithereens. Overkill, if you asked me. There is only one organization that had a vested interest in that thing not being repaired. Their version, according to the scuttlebutt, has been delayed again. It's a year away from completion."

James slumped back in the chair. "Then I'm stuck here."

"You always were stuck here. I wasn't about to fight the FBI to get a plane, that in my opinion, should never have existed. It doesn't matter, however. They are about to screw up the timeline. Everything's going to change. Maybe you'll be a millionaire playboy in the new timeline and live in some penthouse in New York City."

James smiled through his depression. "One could only hope. I just have to wait a year, then try to figure out how they screwed everything up."

"If what Dalton says is true, we won't even know. All this," Ross motioned around the room, "won't even be a distant memory."

"Still, it would have been an awesome thing to have the power to fix everything that's gone bad throughout time. I figured out how to do it, too. Change the past, then go into the future and see how it works out. If it's better, keep the changes, if not, go back and change it back."

Ross chuckled. "You would have been playing Time God. Deciding who lives and who dies. Now someone else will take up the role and I'm sure they don't have the stellar ethics that you possess."

James gave him a sideways glance. "I was going to get rid of a few annoyances along the way. I suppose you're right. I'm not the man to be making those decisions. Still, Time God does have a ring to it."

Ross glanced down at his watch, "Well, Time God, I have to go. Visiting hours are over." He stood up and motioned for the guard to let him out, then shook James' hand. "Take care of yourself."

"It's only for another year," James replied.

When Ross finally came through all the security gates, Williams was waiting for him in the car. "Why do you bother with the man?"

"You should come in with me one of these days. He looks really good in orange." Ross suddenly realized his motivation. He was briefly disappointed with himself.

"I suppose you're right. I would love to see him in orange. I will come in next time."

Both men laughed.

Chapter Nineteen

Seattle, Washington
2046

Jarvin Musktel, Deputy Director of the CIA, looked over the plane. It was finally finished. It was he who had seen the project to completion. He stood beside the two pilots, Ethan Fields and Felix Schmidt. "Well, gentlemen, this is going to be a historic moment. One that history will know nothing about."

Both men milled around the airplane. It was the first time they had seen it. A few practice flights were on the agenda. Most of their training had been in simulators. The CIA didn't want the plane sighted. Too many people would ask too many questions. All tests would be at night. Under no circumstance would they try out the Vmax3 drive. That would only be used for the real thing.

Felix would drop Ethan off in 1970 to destroy the second plane before the hunters found it. That way, the timeline would change and the men who died during the attack on the storage facility would be alive again. Then Felix would travel back to 1912 to find Dalton and destroy the first ship. Only the third ship would survive. There would be a quick stop in 1970 to retrieve Ethan then the two would head back to 2046. There was a safe landing area, close to a bus stop.

The CIA would be the only ones to know about the timeline changes. The two men had with them instructions, signed by Jarvin. If the timeline changes caused him to not know about the mission, they had instructions, signed by him, to debrief the mission so he would be back in the loop. The three of them would keep the missions secret, even from the other CIA agents. Jarvin would select the missions.

The cost of the new airplane had been cleverly disguised as another of Senator James' projects. The plan was to always change the past, then come back to the future to see what changed, then if it was bad, go back in time to change it back if it turned out badly. That way, the timeline would be sculpted the way Jarvin wanted.

The landing and takeoff site would be some land owned by the CIA, but never used. It was within walking distance of a bus stop, so when the missions were over, they just had to open the gate of the fenced off area, and walk to the bus.

Felix was the taller of the two. With straight black hair and a jaw that jutted out, he reminded people of the classic Texas Ranger. Strong and true. Ethan, on the other hand, was balding. Thin as a rail, he stood six inches shorter than Felix. The two men made an odd pair when standing side by side. Both were amazing pilots, and that was all that mattered to Jarvin.

"Well, what do you think?" Jarvin asked.

"Ugly." Felix was stared up at the thing.

"When do we get to fly her?" Ethan sounded eager.

"Soon, very soon. In a few nights, we will start our test flights, then move to the mission. For now, sit in the cockpit and feel the controls. It should be the same as the simulator, but the real McCoy is always a little different."

Both men climbed up the ladders, sitting there for a few minutes before climbing back down. The design was much different than the one Senator James was constructing. Both pilots had the full set of controls. If one of them was disabled, the other had complete control of the airplane.

"Come back in three days. We will move the plane to the property and do the first test flight at the same time," Jarvin ordered.

"I've been wondering," Ethan's voice was hesitant. "What do we do for a ground crew if the shift in the timeline has everyone not knowing who we are?"

"When you clue me back into what's going on, I'll find you a ground crew."

Ethan shrugged. "It's very hard to wrap my mind around how all this works."

"It's uncharted waters. We'll get through it though. If we see a threat to the United States, we'll eliminate it. This is the most powerful weapon ever invented. We can kill the enemy long before they become a threat." Jarvin felt a surge of pride. "Gentlemen, we have a power here that no one else has."

"Except for Senator James and Robert Dalton," Felix corrected.

"Your first mission will change all that. Now get some sleep, history awaits you."

Chapter Twenty

Seattle, Washington
2046

Felix Schmidt sat behind the controls of the Vmax3 airplane. His single status had given him the opportunity to participate in this mission. The fact he could speak German and was a pilot clinched the deal. He had beaten out fifteen other men for the operation.

None of them had been told what it was all about, just that it was a special op. Felix swallowed hard as he thought about it. No one flying this plane had made it back to real time. *They were all stuck in the past.* Now he worried.

The plane was jinxed, it was pure and simple. Jason Ralston was stuck in 1966, Robert Dalton and Gerald Myers in the early 1900s and Phillip Anderson was lost to history in 1970. Where would he end up? Felix wondered. At least he could save Dalton, and maybe Ethan would be able to locate Phillip Anderson. The other two weren't going to make it. There were no plans to rescue them.

Ethan climbed in behind him. Felix hadn't been able to have his friend Jack selected for the operation. The higher-ups wanted Ethan, but the man was just annoying. Felix couldn't stand him. He didn't read the mission briefs, expecting everyone else to interpret them for him. Then he would ask stupid questions about the things he had already been told.

"Are you ready for this?" Ethan asked.

"What, ready for the greatest moment in history? Are you kidding?"

Felix could just picture the cheesy grin on Ethan's face.

When the canopy closed, Felix scanned the area. It was dark and the normally lively airfield was abandoned, except for a couple of men in the tower. It was Christmas Day, the perfect day to fly the new plane away.

Felix spoke into his mike. "Control, this is one-nine-zero, requesting permission to take off."

A bored voice came back. "One-nine-zero, you are cleared for takeoff."

Felix had read about Project Black Hole and how the pilots were heroes, greeted by cheers at each successful point in their operation. This time he would be leaving like a thief in the night.

He throttled the plane up and taxied to the end of the runway. Setting the brakes, he powered to full. When the brakes were released, the plane rolled forward. Unlike most planes, this one was clumsy. It took the entire length of the airstrip to take off. He was under orders not to use the vertical takeoff so as not to alert the tower of the plane's capabilities. Felix doubted they would care.

Once airborne he steered the plane towards the operation area, that's was what they called it anyway. It was a wide spot in the forest. He hovered over it, making sure the system worked before trying to land. Then he began his slow descent to the ground.

Jarvin was there to greet them. He was all smiles as they climbed out of the plane.

"Gentlemen, we did it. Congratulations. Did the plane work perfectly?"

Three men in blue coveralls stood behind Jarvin. They weren't smiling. They were the guys who would be servicing the airplane and they had an unenviable task, given the primitive conditions of the base. Barrels labeled oil and gas were piled up under a shed. A long hose attached to a hand pump delivered the vital liquids to the plane.

Boxes of spare parts occupied the other end of the shed. One building next to the shed looked more like a house than an operations center.

Jarvin and the two pilots retired to the building while the mechanics pulled camouflage netting over the plane.

Once inside, Jarvin turned to Felix. "From now on, you will come in lower and faster when you land here. We don't want to draw any more attention to our location." His words had a bite to them.

Felix was about to explain why he had done it that way, but Ethan cut him off. "How long will we be staying here sir? I need to go shopping."

Felix rolled his eyes, but Jarvin was more patient. "You are assigned here for the duration of the project. You cannot leave. It was all in the briefing we gave you. If you need anything, it will be brought to you."

Ethan's eyes widened. "But I need flowers for my girlfriend."

Even Jarvin shook his head at that. "No," was his simple answer. "Now, gentlemen, get a good night's sleep.

We will fly the plane thirty more times before we become operational."

Chapter Twenty-One

Seattle, Washington
2046

It was another sleepless night for Felix. He could hear Ethan's snoring even through the walls. Having to sleep at the base was only insult to injury. It was because of Ethan's big mouth Jarvin didn't trust them off the base.

The whole mission had been put in jeopardy over him bragging in a bar. No one believed him when he told them he was about to change history. Who knows what he had told that girlfriend of his, the one he wasn't supposed to have. He was selected for the job because he didn't have any attachments. Come to find out, three weeks into training, he had a girlfriend he had kept secret. Jarvin had hit the roof when he found out. The men had been isolated ever since.

Standing it no more, Felix stood up and pounded on the wall.

A muffled, "What? What?" came from the next room.

"Oh, just a hornet on the wall. I got him." Felix smiled. He knew it would take Ethan longer to fall asleep than he would. He hopped back in bed and pulled the covers up over his head.

"Another one? That's the third one tonight."

Felix ignored him and was out cold in a couple of minutes.

Two men in black coats made their way to the front door of the duplex. It was 2 a.m. but they knocked quietly anyway. Both men had guns drawn. A woman in a blue bathrobe answered.

"Well?" the taller of the two asked.

"Not yet. He hasn't sent me flowers. It will be his signal that he has possession of the plane."

"Are you still in contact with him?"

She shook her head. "He's being isolated, but told me he would be able to still send me flowers when the time comes."

"Okay, we'll wait a few more days, but not too many." Both men walked away. The blonde lady shut and locked the door.

The last test flight, Felix brought the plane in just over tree-top level, and dropped it to the ground. It bounced a few feet off the ground and then settled down.

"I hate it when you do that," Ethen complained. "It kills my back." Felix ignored him like he had the more than two dozen other times he had heard the same complaint.

When they climbed out of the plane, Jarvin was all smiles. "That was it, gentlemen, we are now operational. Tomorrow is the real thing. We are going out to celebrate. We'll be going to the finest restaurant in town."

Ethan piped up. "Can I bring my girlfriend?"

"No." Jarvin didn't turn his head to address him. "Go get ready. No suits, but nice resort casual attire."

Both men nodded, then went to their rooms to get dressed.

Jarvin, the two officers and three mechanics all headed into town. It was a chandeliered restaurant with tablecloths and cloth napkins. Something Ethan hated. He was a burger and fries kind of guy. If he wanted to eat fancy, it'd be a chili-cheese dog.

When the first plate came out, he looked down at it. "I don't see the tarter sauce."

Felix ignored him, but Jarvin asked. "What did you order?"

"Tuna in tarter sauce."

Felix snickered to himself. "Tuna tartare, it's raw tuna."

Ethan scowled, "Why couldn't they just put that on the menu instead of writing it in Egyptian."

Felix thought better of continuing the conversation, but Jarvin piped up, "It's French."

"Whatever." Ethan looked down at his plate and gently tasted it, after poking it around for a few minutes. He shrugged his shoulders and ate the rest. "When can I send flowers to my girlfriend?"

"I can't let you leave unattended at this moment, but Sargent Call here can send the flowers for you. Just jot down her name and address and he'll get to the florist in the morning."

Ethan sighed, but found a scrap of paper and wrote down the information. He handed it to the mechanic, who nodded and stuffed it into his pocket.

After dinner, Felix made it his goal for the night to avoid Ethan at all costs. When they arrived back at the base, he went straight to his room. Laying there a couple of hours, not sleeping, he suddenly realized something was different. *No snoring.*

He tiptoed into Ethan's room. The door was open so he peeked in. Ethan wasn't there. He searched the rest of the house for him. Running outside, he scoured the grounds, but couldn't find Ethan anywhere. Running down the road, he noticed the gate was wide open.

Approaching the bus stop on a nearby road, he saw Ethan sitting there. He walked up and sat next to him. Ethen nearly jumped out of his skin.

"The bus doesn't start running till six in the morning."

Ethan, hand still over his thundering heart, said, "Oh."

"Where are you going?"

"I wanted to see my girlfriend just one more time before I left."

Felix shook his head. "Not a possibility. If you come back with me right now, I won't report you to Jarvin. If not, I will raise the alarm, and get you kicked off the program. Either way, you ain't seeing your girlfriend tonight."

Ethan hung his head. "Fine, I'll come back."

Chapter Twenty-Two

Seattle, Washington
2046

Felix scowled at Ethan as they left the command center and headed toward the airplane. After chasing Ethan down the night before, Felix couldn't sleep the next night for all the snoring. He would be leaving Ethan in the 1970s then start the internal debate about picking him back up afterward.

He's a 70s person. He would fit right in. He shook the thoughts out of his mind. He had a mission to do. He didn't need his own thoughts distracting him. The flight suit was clumsy and he was sweating under it.

Jarvin was all smiles as the two approached. He stood next to the plane. "This is it, gentlemen. The day we've all been waiting for." He handed them a manila envelope. "These are your orders. If history changes and I don't remember you, this is what you'll show me so I'll know you're telling me the truth. Good luck."

Felix grunted, took the envelope, and scowled at Ethan again. Not waiting, he climbed the ladder into the plane.

Ethan smiled like a schoolboy at recess. "Thank you Jarvin. It is an exciting moment. The very thought of reshaping time is momentous. I am thankful to be a part of this amazing experiment. Again…"

Felix cut him off. "We need to get going."

"Yes, of course." He shook Jarvin's hand, "Thank you for this opportunity." Then he climbed into the plane.

The plane hummed to life after the canopies were closed. Their makeshift control tower, a small two-story shed packed full of state-of-the-art equipment, radioed the all-clear. The engines vibrated as they lifted the plane higher in the sky.

Felix cringed. Surely someone would hear them. He didn't like early morning flights. People would be asleep or too tired to look if they heard a sound at night, but during the daylight, all they had to do was turn their head that direction.

The scattered farmland lay below them. Jarvin had told them not to worry. "Farmers are too busy to worry about planes." It didn't help. He still felt very exposed.

He quickly brought the plane to a higher altitude than normal, pointed it forward, and accelerated.

"Slow down there, jet jockey," Ethan complained from the back seat.

"Set the Vmax drive and get us out of this century," Felix barked back.

Ethan mumbled a, "Yes, Sir," as he worked the controls. Then in a cheerier tone, he said, "1970, here we come."

The two men were back at her door. She opened reluctantly. "No flowers."

The taller one shook his head. "Flowers or no flowers, we can't wait. We're going in."

"But he said he would send flowers."

Both men turned and walked away without answering.

Jarvin Musktel slept soundly that night, a thing he did rarely, but he could finally relax. The mission had gone off without a hitch, despite knowing there was a mole somewhere. The barrel of a pistol against his temple woke him with a start. "What?"

"Don't move," said the gruff voice.

Jarvin glanced sideways at his wife. Another man stood by her bedside but hadn't woken her. He hissed, "What do you want?"

"Get up. We need to talk."

His wife opened her eyes, but before she could move, she had a gloved hand clapped over her mouth and a pistol pointed at her face. "Not one sound, or you die right here and now, do you understand?"

Wide-eyed, she nodded at the man standing over her. He slowly moved his hand.

"The other man motioned Jarvin into the next room. "You, come with me. She stays here."

They walked over to the kitchen, where two more men were waiting for them.

The taller one smiled as he entered the room. "Jarvin Musktel, I'm Special Agent Gardner of the FBI. Please sit down." He pulled out one of the kitchen chairs, but Jarvin shook his head.

The man with a gun pushed him down into it anyway. "That was not a request. That was an order."

"What do you want? This is an illegal kidnapping. You can't do this," Jarvin blurted out.

"It seems that the rules have changed." Gardner's smile disappeared. "When the CIA starts killing FBI agents, then all bets are off the table. According to our director, we now have an open season on you and your men. Tell me, sir, where is the Vmax3 plane?"

"I don't know what you're talking about."

Gardner called out to the man in the other room, "John."

A shot rang out. His wife screamed.

Jarvin stood up and lunged for Gardner. The other man intercepted him. They sprawled across the floor. Jarvin trying to get up, but the third man in the room helped hold him down.

After a few minutes, Jarvin was handcuffed and thrown back onto the chair, his legs panduited to the chair legs.

"Let's try this again. Where is the Vamx3 plane?" Gardner had stood there calmly even when the fight was taking place.

Jarvin could hear his wife's whimpers from the other room. "It's at the Gilman property. A CIA base of operations. You're too late. The mission has started already. The plane took off yesterday morning."

Gardner's eyes widened. "Let's go," he yelled, and two men followed him out the door.

The other one shot Jarvin, then fled.

Gardner sat in the forest, close enough to see the gate but still not be spotted by those inside the fence. A drone hovered overhead. Its silent motors on gray paint made it particularly difficult to spot on this cloudy day.

The armored vehicle idled beside the road. It sat next to the command post. Gardner walked back down the road and to the command post. Two men watched the monitors intently. "What do we have?"

The one monitoring the drone looked up. "Low security. Four armed guards and a half a dozen technicians. It looks as though they haven't been alerted."

"Go in."

The armored vehicle revved its engine and accelerated rapidly, crashing through the gate. Bullets flew from all directions, pinging off the truck.

"It's a trap. They were waiting for us. Call in more men and drones," Gardner screamed through his microphone.

Five military drones appeared overhead. The armored truck tried to back out, but it was hit with an RPG and blew up. Men dashed out of the back, only to be cut down.

The drones let loose their missiles. Explosions erupted all through the base almost simultaneously. The control room burst into flame. Men on fire ran out, desperate to get away. Two more armored vehicles rushed through the gate and disgorged more men.

A few minutes later, an agent climbed inside the command post. "Sir, they're all dead. The base is ours."

"How many were there?"

"Twenty."

Garner shook his head. "And how many did we lose?"

"The eight in the first truck are all dead, four others wounded. It doesn't matter. When we get the plane, we'll change the timeline. They'll all be alive again soon."

Chapter Twenty-Three

Issaquah, Washington
1970

The plane set down in a clearing next to where the second Vmax3 airplane was discovered. Felix and Ethan didn't know the timeline as to when it had originally crashed but knew an approximate. They both had machine pistols.

Crawling over the hill, the two men spied out the clearing where Vmax number two was supposed to be. It wasn't there.

"Well, I guess you're waiting here for it," Felix smiled.

"It could be years," Ethan protested. He knew Felix was relishing the thought of leaving him.

"Nonsense, they find the plane in six months. It sat here for a few months before being discovered. It should be any day now."

"But," was all Ethan could get out.

Felix marched back up to the plane, handed Ethen the mission bag, and with a wave, he took off.

Sitting down in a dejected heap, Ethan looked through his package. He had the explosives to blow up the plane, the gun, the information to give back to Jarvin, and enough 70s era cash to last him months. All he needed was a plane to blow up. *How does he know when to pick me up?* The thought brought shivers down his spine.

After sitting there for hours, he decided to walk into the nearest town. He checked into a cheap motel, stowed his bag under the bed, and walked over to grab some food. All he could find was a restaurant bar, combination on the edge of town. Walking in, he was met with a cloud of smoke. Everyone in the place seemed to have a lit cigarette.

Coughing a little as he made his way to a table, he sat down. The waitress, without a word, dropped off a menu. He perused it, but didn't even know what some of this stuff was. *Chicken a la King?* It didn't sound edible, so he ordered a hamburger instead.

A woman sat herself down at his table. "I thought I knew every patron in this bar, but I ain't never seen you before." She had dirty blonde hair with a nice complexion and smile.

"I'm only passing through." He took another bite of his hamburger.

She motioned to the nearest waitress, "Emma, we'll have two beers here."

"Sure, Annie."

"I'm Annie Harris. What's your name, Honey?"

"Ethan."

"Ethan, that's a funny sounded name. I ain't never met an Ethan before. You got a last name, Ethan?"

"Fields."

"You one of the Fields from Sammamish Plateau?"

"No, never heard of the place. I'm from Seattle." He leaned back in his seat when the beers came and took a sip. "You?"

"Oh, big city folk. You got a girl?"

"Not in this…" He caught himself and let out an embarrassed laugh.

She folded her arms, "Were you going to say, not in this town?"

He laughed louder. "No. I was going to say, not in this century."

She giggled. "You are a strange one. What do you mean by that?"

"I mean, I'm not from around here, time-wise." He took a long draw from his beer. "I'm from the future. I've come to destroy a time machine."

She stared at him for a minute. "Now I've heard everything." Her forehead creased. "You're here to destroy a time machine? That don't make any sense. Didn't you have to come in a time machine? Now you're going to destroy it? I'm confused."

"I have a motel room next door. Perhaps I can explain it to you. Might take all night."

"Hmm," she cocked her head. "I thought I'd heard every pick-up line. That's a new one on me. Perhaps you can tell me about this future of yours. That might be a story, but what a story."

He paid for his bill and escorted her to his room.

In the morning, she followed him to look to see if the Vmax3 plane was there yet. They crawled up over the hill, but it hadn't arrived.

"You sure it's going to be here? Maybe you got the place wrong," Annie said.

"Positive. It should be here in a day or two."

"If you want to tell me it was all a big joke, I'll still like you." She stood there with her hands on her hips.

"I'm telling you the truth. You'll see, it'll look just like I described it."

She laughed. "I ain't never met a man like you. Okay, here's the deal. You buy me lunch, then I got to get to work. I'll come back tomorrow to see you. If your time machine ain't here by then, I ain't gonna believe you anymore."

"Okay, but I can't guarantee that it'll be here tomorrow, either."

She folded her arms. "That's the deal."

Chapter Twenty-Four

Issaquah, Washington
1970

A knock on the door woke Ethan. He pulled his pants on and opened it. Annie stood there. "Did you hear that rumble this morning?" she asked.

"I must've slept right through it." He slipped on his shirt on and grabbed his shoes.

"Ya, I thought it was thunder at first, but it was long and steady like, but grew louder, then stopped altogether."

His eyes widened. "That wasn't thunder. I think it was the time machine." He grabbed the explosives and ran towards the clearing. She followed as best she could. He slowed down when he arrived at the edge of it. She was out of breath when she caught up to him.

The Vmax3 plane sat there in front of them.

"Wow!" she blurted out.

"Shh, I don't want the pilot to figure out we're here. I told you. That's the time machine." He whispered.

They ducked behind a tree when Phillip Anderson climbed out of the plane to check the damage. "Dalton," he screamed, shaking his fist in the air.

"Who's Dalton?" Annie whispered.

"The guy he was sent back to 1912 to get. Dalton must have shot up the airplane. That's why it didn't make it back to my century."

"Oh."

They waited until Phillip left the area. "I'm going to leave the detonator up here. I don't want to accidentally set it off. Don't touch the red button."

"Okay."

He ran down to set charges. When he was done, he started to climb back up the hill.

"What are you doing?"

Ethan turned around to see Phillip standing behind him.

"I've got to blow it up. It'll destroy the future if I don't."

"No!" Phillip held up his pistol. "Get away from the plane."

"I've got to destroy it." He looked up at the hillside and with a fist, moved his thumb up and down.

Annie grabbed the detonator.

Three shots rang out. Annie gasped. Looking down, she saw Ethan on the ground bleeding. Phillip turned his head to look up the hill. She pushed the button.

A huge fireball erupted from the clearing. She was blown back five feet by the force of the explosion. She lay there for a few minutes. Scanning herself, she didn't notice any bleeding. Her ears ringing and a large fire burned around the wreckage of the plane. She heard sirens approaching. Not wanting to be seen there, she ran down the other side of the hill.

When she arrived at her house, she looked in the mirror. Her face was black with smoke, but her eyelashes and brows weren't burnt off. She took a quick shower.

Returning to the motel where Ethan was staying, she knocked on the door.

"Hi, Annie," the tall, heavy-set manager said.

"Hi, Bruce. I need the key to room five."

"Is that funny-talking guy going to come back? The guy from space."

She grinned. "You mean, from the future? No, he skipped town. Got into some trouble in the woods."

He turned around and grabbed the key for her. "Here you go."

She opened the door and went through all of his stuff. *Ten thousand dollars. This guy was loaded.* She kept the gun and the money, then headed out the door. She stopped in the doorway. *The mattress, I almost forgot the mattress.* Sliding her hand between the mattress and box spring, she found over five thousand more. *They always hide stuff under the mattress.*

Peeling off some bills, she made her way back to the office. "Great news, Bruce. He had a thousand dollars on him. Here's your share. Keep those tips coming." She handed him four hundred.

"Wow, that's great. This is our best haul yet."

"Yes, it is."

When she arrived home, she stuffed most of the cash in the shut-off heater vent. It was her chance to escape this small town and go on to the big time. "Las Vegas, here I come."

Jumping on the bed, she threw a handful of bills into the air and let them float down onto her.

The plane! She suddenly remembered. Turning on the news, she listened to the report.

"There's been a plane crash outside of Issaquah, Washington. Two badly burned bodies were recovered from the wreckage. It is believed that they are the pilots of the aircraft."

Poor Ethan.

Chapter Twenty-Five

The Hamptons, New York
1913

Not again. Dalton was jarred awake by the sound of the Vmax3 Jet landing. In his dreams, it happened over and over again. This time he wasn't dreaming.

Mary sat bolt upright in bed. "It's them again."

"Go get David. Tell him, 'it's time.'"

She ran down the hall, stopping at Bryan's room to collect the crying child, before waking David.

Dalton ran out the back door to confront the pilot. He was suddenly staring down the face of a machine pistol.

"R. Adalwolf Dalton, I presume. Or should I just call you Major?"

Dalton raised his arms. David would need time. He knew he had to stall. "Who do I have the pleasure of meeting?"

"Felix Schmidt, CIA."

"That's funny, the CIA doesn't exist yet."

Felix smiled, "They will."

"What can I do for you, Agent Schmidt?"

"My job is to destroy the time machine in this century, so there is nothing to be found and rebuilt."

Dalton nodded. "So, the CIA would have the only useable copy of the machine. I see. Destroying the time machine is a great idea. That's what I'd like to do also. But I want to destroy all copies of it."

The machine gun on the other side of the yard, came to life. It sprayed bullets from one end of the plane to the other. Felix turned towards David and raised his gun. It was too late. Dalton tackled him. Wrestling the pistol away from him, Dalton stood up. "Raise your hands."

Felix complied. "You can't let him destroy it. I want to get back to my own time. Stop him."

Dalton shrugged. "It isn't so bad."

The machine gun stopped. David came running around the front of the plane. "I did it, Uncle Adalwolf. I blasted it." Just then he noticed Felix, arms raised. "Oh, hello. Welcome to the 20th Century."

Felix hung his head. "I can't believe you did this. I had a mission. I left a man in the seventies, I need to go get him. This can't be happening."

Dalton motioned with his gun. "Over against that tree. David, tie him up."

"You've drawn a lot of attention." Felix wasn't giving in. "You can't have me tied to a tree when the neighbors come and investigate. They'll wonder what that machine is and why you're kidnapping someone."

Dalton smiled. "Luckily, there aren't a lot of neighbors. Those we do have, are used to the sound of a Vickers machine gun, as David and I play with it a lot. They even join us from time to time. Their only complaint in the morning will be the early hour in which we fired it. That's not going to make them happy." Dalton motioned again. "Get over there."

Felix complied and soon he was tied up. "What are you going to do with the plane? A lot of people will see it in the morning."

"You just don't give up, do you." David pulled open the barn doors. The barn was empty except for some hay in the loft to make the thing look like a real barn. "You see, we've been expecting you. Only, you didn't land where we thought you would."

Both Dalton and David ran to the shed and drove back out with large tractors. Tying ropes around the plane, they pulled the machine into the barn, then covered it up.

Dalton walked over to Felix. "We're going to destroy it. The most important bit is the Vmax3 drive. I'm going to dismantle it bit by bit and melt the thing down. There will be nothing left. We have a World War just around the corner. We're going to need lots of metal."

"Let me out. I have no reason to resist you now. I'm stuck in time, just like you are."

"I'm going to drive you to the center of New York before I release you. I don't want you anywhere near me and my family."

They threw him in the back of the car. It was dawn before they let him go. Dalton gave Felix back his flight jacket. He stood there and watched Dalton drive off. Felix wasn't dressed in period clothes. The mission should have been a quick land and grab. He was very out of place in his olive drab flight suit.

Poor Ethan. The thought struck him as strange. He never liked the man. Why would he have sympathy for him? Felix was a lot worse off, time-wise. Then he realized, *He's going to wait in vain.* The morning was chilly, so he put his jacket on. As he felt in the pocket, he realized Dalton had put some bills in there. *A thousand. That'll come in handy.*

Chapter Twenty-Six

New York, New York
1913

Felix sat in a café looking out on the Brooklyn Bridge. Horse-drawn carriages outnumbered cars by about three to one. Trolleys were the main occupants of the bridge, as they scooted across it. Steamships and pleasures vessels sailed under it. Once in a while he saw a fully rigged clipper ship slide by.

Thinking he might as well be on another planet than this time. It couldn't be more alien. He mumbled under his breath, "Curse you, Dalton."

"More coffee?"

He looked up to see a smiling waitress standing over him. "Oh, yes, please."

The thin waitress, pencil in her hair, poured as she asked, "Who's Dalton?"

"My arch enemy number one."

"Oh, dear, Life's too short to be angry at someone. Make them a friend."

Felix thought about it for a minute. "You're right. I like that idea. Thank you, I'll do that."

She smiled and walked away.

He watched her as she made her way from table to table. Despite her occupation, she moved around like a princess, her head held high, and a grace he hadn't seen in a woman for many years. When she walked back up to his table, he checked for rings. There were none.

Getting his nerve up when she gave him the check, he said, "What's your number? We should get together sometime. I'm new here in town and don't have anyone to talk to."

She stood there for a moment. "Number? I don't think I have any numbers. You mean, how much was the tab?"

"No, your telephone number."

"Telephone? I've heard about that. Don't have one of them. It's only for the rich and I'm not one of those." She walked away.

That went well. He sighed.

He walked out into the street, wondering where he was going to sleep. He spied a hotel sign a couple of blocks down. It was nothing to write home about, a plain room with a single bed, not much more than a cot, and a shared bathroom down the hall. He looked in the mirror and saw his flight suit. No wonder everyone was looking at him strangely. He had to get some real clothes. He took off his jacket and lay down.

Strange dreams plagued him. In two of his dreams, Dalton shot him at close range. He woke three times to the sound of the machine gun in his mind. He stood up and looked out the window. Wiping it with his hand first to get some of the grime off, he looked down on the streets of New York. Tall buildings on either side of the street, people going to work, chasing after streetcars, most successfully, some not.

Horses weren't a stranger to the streets either. He watched several clippidy-clop, by pulling a carriage, or just having a rider on them. A few cars also drove by. Several of them even had chauffeurs.

"I'm in a history book. Curse you, Dalton."

Going downstairs, he headed to the same diner he ate at the night before.

When he sat down, the waitress came and poured him some coffee.

"You work nights and mornings?"

She gave him a sideways glance. "No, I just work mornings. My sister works nights."

"Oh. Are you twins?"

She smiled, "No, we just look a lot alike. She's my older sister. We both work for Daddy."

"Thank you."

When his order arrived, he began to eat. The waitress came back and filled his coffee. "Do you like my sister? She needs a good man in her life, after the divorce and all. Are you a good man, mister?"

"Annie, you have other customers," a voice called out from over the counter. She hustled away.

When she brought the bill, she looked over her shoulder, then whispered, "She's a really good woman. Daddy makes her work nights so he can keep an eye on her, but she needs a man in her life."

"Good to know. Do you know where I can find an apartment in the area?"

A man walked up behind the waitress. He was bald with a two-day beard. His face was formed into a perma-frown. "What's going on here?" His deep voice drew everyone's attention.

"He's only asking where there's an apartment to rent around here, Daddy."

The man pointed to the left. "Two blocks down, on the left."

"Are they nice?" Felix asked.

"No, if you want nice, you'll have to go to the right, five blocks."

"Thank you."

The man grabbed the waitress' arm and led her away.

Chapter Twenty-Seven

New York, New York
1913

As he walked down the street, everyone was staring at him. Felix ducked into a men's clothing store. An hour later, he emerged with a black suit, bow tie, and a bowler hat. Now as he walked around, no one stared. He walked the five blocks to the right. In front of him stood a large building that shot straight up from the sidewalk. Lots of windows dotted the exterior. He walked in. "I'm looking for an apartment."

"I have just the thing for you. Let me show you the way." The manager, complete with suit and tails, oiled down hair and pencil-thin mustache, led Felix up the five flights of stairs.

"No elevator?" Felix huffed. He was out of breath by the time they reached the top.

"Oh, no. Not in a short building like this."

"I see." He opened the curtains to a view of the waterfront. "Wow." Clippers and full-rigged brigantines dotted the harbor. A steamer drifted past as he watched.

"Not much to look at, only the ships coming and going, but I suppose it's better than nothing."

"I'll take it." He hadn't seen the rest of the apartment.

"Very well. That will be five hundred."

Felix swung around. "A month!"

"Heavens no. That is for the year."

"Oh." Felix pulled out the bills and counted them out into the man's palm.

"I'll be back with your receipt."

As the door shut, Felix walked through every room, a kitchen, fully stocked with pots and pans, all of which looked new, a couch that belonged in a museum. In fact, all the furniture did. It was ornately carved wood with satin fabric. No carpeting, but throw rugs covered most of the wood floor. The bed had dark wood paneling at the head and the foot.

He wandered some more. "Where's the bathroom?" He opened the door to what he thought was a closet. "Whew." It had a sink and a toilet with the tank near the ceiling. A chain off the side of the tank dangled down. The seat was made of wood.

"I hope there are no splinters." *I'm talking to myself. I must be losing it.*

After the tour, he went to lie down. He hadn't slept much in the cot the night before. A knock on the door stopped him. He answered it and was given a receipt by the manager. "Thank you."

The manager just grunted and made his way down the stairs.

Deciding he was hungrier than he was tired, he headed back to the restaurant. The same waitress was there, or was it her sister? He couldn't tell. He sat down at the same table he had before.

"What can I get you?" she asked.

"I'll have a steak and a beer."

She checked the clock on the wall. "No, too early for beer. How about a Coca-Cola?"

"No, please bring me a water. Coca-Cola still has cocaine in it at this point in time." His eyes widened when he realized what he'd said.

"At four o'clock? Will it change as the night progresses?"

He laughed, "I just want ice water."

"No ice, but I do have water. I recognize you now. You were the one in the clown suit yesterday. Nice to see you in real clothes."

"It's a flight suit, not a clown suit, but it was out of place in the city."

"A flight suit? What are you a bird? I didn't see any feathers."

He looked at the guy behind the counter. He was frowning, but not saying anything. This daughter seemed to have more leeway when it came to talking to customers.

"No, I'm a pilot. I fly airplanes."

"Oh, I thought only the military and the Wright brothers had airplanes. Are you in the Signal Corps?"

"No."

She gave him a wry smile. "Then you're not really a pilot, are you? Just trying to impress the girl?"

"The plane I flew was top secret. You wouldn't have heard about it."

She glanced at him sideways. "I like you. You get caught in a lie and you keep going with it. You just don't give up, do you?"

He leaned forward. "Maybe, just maybe, I'm not lying."

"Hmmf. I'll get the cook to start your steak, flyboy."

He leaned back, feeling he had won that round. She came back a little while later and plunked down the steak and a glass of water in front of him. "I'm Diana. Do you have a name, flyboy?"

"Felix, like the cat?"

She leaned back. "What cat?"

"Felix the cat. The cartoon?"

"Never heard of it."

He looked down. "It may not be a thing yet. Never mind."

"A thing? You do talk strangely. Where are you from?"

"San Bernardino, California."

"You're a long way from home. How did you come to be here?"

"I came in an airplane. One that crashed. It can't be fixed so I'm stuck here."

She laughed. "You're no longer a pilot then. You have no plane."

"I'm still a pilot. I don't need a plane to be a pilot."

She put her finger on her chin. "Let me see, if someone flew a plane from California to New York City, you'd think I'd have heard it on the radio. I didn't."

"I flew from Washington State, but remember, it was a top-secret plane."

She pointed at him. "You have me there. Enjoy your meal."

Round two to Felix. He smiled.

Chapter Twenty-Eight

New York, New York
1913

Dalton stewed and stormed for a week. *Are they going to send another one? Will they rescue me out of the water? I'd go if they rescued me out of the water or off that ship.* Things had changed since he was on the ship. *How many planes do they have, anyway?*

He should have talked to Felix longer. He just wanted to get rid of the guy. The neighbors complained about the firing of the machine gun in the middle of the night. He apologized. That was the end of it.

Mary put her arm around him. "They have to run out of planes eventually, don't they?"

"I have to destroy the first one. They won't copy it if it's destroyed. Phillip said it was Ted that found it. I need to find him and stop him."

"Don't stop him. Someone else will figure it out eventually. No, you have to destroy it."

He thought about it for a minute. "You're right. I have to get there first. I should have asked Felix what year Ted pulls the plane from the ocean."

"He can't have traveled far. He should be around the area you dropped him off."

"New York is a large place. It's hard to find a needle in a haystack, even if you know about where the needle is."

"What are you going to do then?"

"I can't do much until the war is over, but afterward, I'll destroy the machine. Meanwhile, I need to start melting the one in the barn down."

Felix went shopping at the street market around the corner from his new apartment. He couldn't believe how quickly he was going through the money Dalton had given him. He needed a job, any job. It would allow him to invest the rest of the money instead of spending it. He knew just who to invest it in also. Then he would write a book or do something else to make himself famous. People in the future would know who he was and come rescue him when they built another time machine.

He went down to the diner. He had to stop eating out every night. It was taking too much money, but he wanted to see the girl again.

The restaurant was nearly empty when he walked in. Choosing his usual table, he sat down. Both sisters were there this time. Standing side by side, he could tell them apart. Diana was a little taller than her younger sister. It was the other one that came to his table though.

"Can I help you?"

"I was hoping Diana would be my server."

"Nope, this is my table during lunch."

"Where are Diana's tables? I'll sit at one of those."

She rolled her eyes. "Never mind, I'll go get her."

She whispered something in Diana's ear, and then walked away.

"Something wrong with Cindy? You don't like her?"

"No, I just like you better."

She suppressed a smile. "You are forward, aren't you, Felix?"

"I don't mean to be, it's just that I really enjoyed our conversation the other day."

"Oh, well, thank you. What can I get you?"

"I'll have the chicken sandwich and the onion soup."

"A very good choice."

She turned to go back to the counter. "Wait," he said. "I can't afford to eat here every meal. Do you know where a guy could find a job?"

"I do. We have a problem keeping dishwashers. Are you up to that. Twenty cents an hour and free food."

"I'll take it."

A few minutes later, the man behind the counter came and sat at his table after putting the food down. "I'm Harry. I understand you're our new dishwasher."

"I guess so. When can I start?"

"There's a stack of dishes back there now. I'd have to do them before I went home, but with you here, I won't." Harry glared at him. "It's a desperate man that washes dishes just to meet a girl. What's your interest in my daughter?"

Felix swallowed. "I like your daughter. I would like to get to know her better."

"Her heart's been broken before. I don't want to see it broken again. Are you just passing through, or are you going to stick around a while?"

"I'm stuck here, I'm afraid. I'll be here for a long time."

Harry nodded. "Enjoy your meal."

Chapter Twenty-Nine

New York, New York
1913

Felix was up to his elbows in suds when Diana walked into the kitchen. "Dry off, Daddy's given us the rest of the day off."

He was fine with working hard. The free food and the company of Diana and Cindy made his days complete. He rinsed then dried his hands. "What's the occasion?"

"The diner is slow today. Cindy wants to work late so she can have tomorrow off, so we get to go out on the town."

"Great, let me get my jacket."

The two went arm in arm down the street. As they passed a restaurant, Diana sighed. "I've always wanted to eat there."

"Why don't you then?"

She shook her head. "Women don't go to such places unaccompanied."

He shook his head. "Really? That sounds so archaic. Where I come from, women could not only eat where and when they wanted, they ran a lot of the restaurants."

"In California?"

He swallowed. "It's not so much a place, but a time. I can't say more."

"You do talk in riddles."

"May I accompany you to this fine establishment?" He gave her a mock bow.

"Really, could we go in? I would love that. Listen, I can pay, if you can't afford it, I mean."

"I can afford it." He smiled.

She took his arm and they both walked in the door. The host nodded. "Do you have reservations?"

"I didn't know I needed them."

"Let me see." The host flipped the page. "Oh, yes. We've had a cancellation. I do have a table for you."

"That would be wonderful."

As they sat down, the waiter brought them the menus. Diana gasped. "This place is hugely expensive. I didn't know it was this bad. We can leave if you want to."

"It's fine. If I can't afford the bill, I can always wash dishes."

She giggled.

A man standing over the table drew their attention.

Dalton glared down at him. "I need to talk to you. Don't leave the restaurant." Then he went and sat down at a nearby table.

"Who's that?"

Felix felt pale. He wondered what Dalton wanted and how he had tracked him down.

"Who's that?" she asked again.

"Major Robert Dalton of the United States Air Force. He goes by Adalwolf in this century though."

"Air Force? This century? What are you talking about? What's going on?"

"I'll tell you later. Right now, the food looks divine. We'll worry about the Major afterward."

She took a deep breath. "Oh, okay. You'll explain later."

They ordered and enjoyed their meal. When they left the restaurant, Dalton was waiting for them outside. "What year does Ted pull the plane from the ocean floor?"

"1925."

"Okay, that gives me some time. How did he find it?"

"Fishermen would go around it, so as not to lose their nets. What about me?"

Mary gazed over at Diana. The poor girl was wide-eyed, listening to the men. Mary patted her hand. "There, there, dear."

"If it's destroyed, will I go back to my own time? I mean, with the timeline change."

"No, the timeline change doesn't affect you. You're here, there's no way you'll get back once the plane is destroyed."

"I see," Felix replied. "Thank you, Major. How did you find me?"

"I wasn't looking. I just happen to be eating here when you walked in. Mary and I come into the city once a week on the train for a night out."

"What happens now?"

"Well, we have to get through the first World War, then I get the plane before the depression hits. How are you doing for money?"

"I have a little less than half of what you gave me. I've settled down and gotten a job though so I'm not going through it very fast."

Dalton reached into his jacket and pulled out his wallet. "Here's another five hundred. That should tide you over for a while. Where are you working?"

"A diner down the street. I'm the dishwasher."

"You go from flying time machines to washing dishes." Dalton shook his head. "If you need a better job, let me know."

"Will do, Sir."

Dalton and Mary left the couple in the middle of the street.

Chapter Thirty

New York, New York
1913

"You're leaving? World war? 1925? Great Depression? What's happening? What was that conversation all about? Who walks up and hands someone five hundred dollars?"

He held out his hands to stop her. "Whoa, one question at a time."

She drew a deep breath. "You're leaving?" She put her hands on her hips.

"No, I'm not leaving and I wouldn't have left without you anyway."

"So, where are we going, and who asked me if I wanted to go with you?"

"It's not a place, it's a time."

Her eyes widened. "What time?"

"I guess it doesn't matter. There is no reason to keep it secret anymore. I'm not from this century."

"What?"

"It hard to explain. That was Major Dalton."

"The man you hate?"

"Well, yes and no. He is the reason I'm here, but he's willing to help me out."

"Five hundred dollars' worth."

"Well, more than that. Anyway. I can't believe I'm telling you this. Dalton was sent on a mission to let a bad man die. He failed. I was sent to find out why he failed and bring him back. He destroyed the vehicle I traveled in, so I'm stuck here."

Folding her arms, she said, "Go on."

"That thing was a time machine."

"Oh, like the one H. G. Wells wrote about."

"Yes," he smiled. "Only it's real. It's an airplane. I flew it here from Washington state to bring Dalton back with me, only he didn't want to come. He destroyed the time machine. There is another one on the bottom of the ocean that will be found later on by a man named Ted. Dalton wants to destroy that one too."

"I don't believe a word you're saying." She turned around and stomped away.

The next day at work, Diana gave him the cold shoulder. Cindy came back to the kitchen. "Did you two have a lover's spat? You aren't talking to each other."

"I ran into an old friend. She didn't like what we were saying to each other. I tried to make it better, but it only made it worse."

"She never stays mad. Give her a day or two."

Felix was tired at quitting time. He walked down the street and headed toward his apartment, not noticing Diana was following him.

"Tell me the truth."

He turned to face her. "About what?"

"Let's start with who are you?"

"Felix Schmidt. I work for the CIA."

She stepped closer. "What's the CIA?"

"Central Intelligence Agency. Don't bother looking it up. It doesn't exist yet."

"How can you work for something that doesn't exist?"

"It does exist in my time."

She glared. "Now you're talking in riddles."

"I was born in the year 2016 in California. I was hired by the CIA because I was a pilot. A very good pilot. They needed someone to fly an airplane with a time machine in it. There were two of us. I left the other man in the 1970s. He's now stuck in that time. I came here to get Dalton, but he was expecting me and destroyed my time machine."

She stared at him for a few minutes, then said. "That's impossible."

"I can't prove it to you." He held up a hand, "Wait, I can too. My cell phone. I turned it off because I couldn't charge it in this century, but it should have enough battery power left to show you it. Come with me."

He walked to his apartment. She reluctantly followed. When he walked through the door, she stayed in the hall.

"It's not proper to be alone with a man in a flat."

"Okay, I'll bring it to you."

Walking back into the hall, he showed her the phone. "This is a cell phone. It can talk to other cell phones. You carry it with you so people can get a hold of you."

She picked it up and looked at all sides. "Show me how it works."

When he turned it on she nearly jumped out of her skin. It vibrated and beeped. "Here is the home screen. A lot of these things I can't do because there are no cell towers in this century. But I have some game apps." He showed her a couple of games on it. She stood there wide-eyed.

"How can it do all that?"

"It must look like magic to you, but in my century, everyone has one of these, including school children. My battery power is down to twenty percent. I have to turn it off."

"I don't know if I believe you yet, but I'm more open to it now that I've seen that."

"I'll put this back and then walk you home."

Heading down the stairs and leaving out the front door, she commented, "Other things that Dalton said have been bothering me. For instance, what's this about a World War? The First World War he called it."

"The Great War. That's what they'll call it. The war to end all wars. It's so bad that millions of people die. The whole landscape of Europe is changed. It was so bad they said they'd never be another war, but the Second World War starts around twenty years later. It was worse than the first."

She put her hand to her heart. "My goodness. How can countries be so stupid to start a war so big?"

"It will start small. Archduke Ferdinand will get assassinated by a separatist. That's what starts the first war. The second one, historians say, was a continuation of the first."

She stopped walking and looked him in the eye. "You can stop it. You know how it begins. You can keep it from happening. You can save millions of lives."

"I can't. I know how this timeline ends up. I don't know how it would change. It could be far worse. Anyway, the countries of Europe are wanting to go at each other. If they don't use Ferdinand as an excuse, they'll find another."

She started walking again, but much slower than the first time. "I don't understand. How could it be worse than the whole world at war."

"It wasn't the whole world, just most of it."

Chapter Thirty-One

The next day at work, Diana came back to the kitchen to quiz Felix again. "What is the Great Depression that Dalton talked about?"

"It's where the stock market crashes and a lot of businesses will go bankrupt. The unemployment rate skyrockets with lots and lots of people are out of work."

"How can we stop that?"

His felt his face flush. "We can't, nor are we going to try. History has to take its course. It's bad, but it could be worse."

"It could be better, too. We can stop a lot of the suffering. If we can stop the suffering, why wouldn't we try?"

He shook his head. "It's good that you believe me, but we can't change history. We barely survive in the timeline we end up in."

She stomped her foot. "Right, we barely survive, you said it yourself. I want a history we can thrive in. We can stop the World War, we can stop the Great Depression. Think about all of the things we can stop. We have to try." She turned and marched out.

Felix finished his shift, dried off his hands and headed towards the door.

"Wait a minute." Harry, Diana's father blocked his way to the door. "Here's your pay for the last two weeks. You do a good job."

"Thank you, Sir."

"I have to tell you one thing, before you get too serious with Diana. She's a divorcee." Harry stood there like he was expecting a bad reaction, some facial expression that would show Felix's disapproval.

"I knew that already."

"How did you know that? Oh, Cindy."

"Yes. I have no problem with it."

"Good. I see a drive in her that I haven't seen in a while. She's alive and passionate, like she has something to live for. Keep up the good work."

"Thank you, I will."

As he stepped outside Diana was waiting for him. "I saw you and Daddy talking. What did you find to talk about?"

"You."

"Humph, what about me?"

"He's being protective. Tell me about this previous marriage. You haven't talked about him at all."

"We had a nice little apartment on the east side. I was deeply in love, but all he talked about was going to sea. One day, he left without a word. I was devastated. I waited and waited for him to return, but he never did, so I filed for divorce."

"You never found out what happened to him?"

"Yes, I know. He left me."

On his off hours, Felix went down to the library and studied up on companies that built ships and manufactured munitions. He then invested his left-over money in those industries.

The snow flew as winter held its grip on the eastern seaboard. That didn't stop Diana. She wanted to know more. One day, after work, she took Felix aside. "I need to talk to Dalton. Do you know where he lives?"

"I don't know if that's a good idea. He'd be very upset at me for telling you all this."

"He would love all the good I can do with the knowledge he can give me. Please, take me to him."

He knew it was a bad idea, but found himself saying, "Yes," to the pleading eyes.

Two days later, on a Sunday when the restaurant was closed, he bought a couple of train tickets to the Hamptons. It was a blustery day, and the snow covered over some of the landmarks he tried to use to get back to Dalton's house, but after few inquiries with the neighbors and he found it.

When he knocked on the door, David answered.

"Uncle, it's the guy from the future and he brought a girl with him."

Dalton scowled when he reached the door. "What are you doing back here?"

Felix opened his mouth to answer, but Diana spoke first. "I want to use your knowledge of the future to save mankind from devastating wars and financial difficulties."

Dalton looked at her, then looked back at Felix, then looked at her again. He sighed, "Come in."

He led them through the entryway and into the living room. He bid them sit. A few minutes later, Mary came out with coffee and pastries and set them down before them.

When they were all settled, Dalton looked deep into Diana's eyes and said, "We can't change the future without destroying the timeline."

"But, we can stop bad things from happening."

"Yes, but what if we make it worse? I let a little boy die. He would grow up to be a monster, so they had me go back in time to stop his rescuer from saving him. When I came back to the present, the war I tried to prevent was still going on. Billions had died instead of millions. I went back and restored the timeline. The millions who had died were better than the billions who were going to. You can't change the timeline without a way to fix it if it all goes wrong. I don't have a way to fix it, so I won't change it."

"But we could do so much good."

He shook his head. "You're not listening to me. That little boy you save, what will become of him when he grows up? Will he be a regular person, or will he cause worldwide destruction? We don't know. It's an unknown. If you save ten, then you have ten unknowns. Will they change the timeline for the better or the worse? You can multiply that unknown by a thousand, or a million. You have that many more unknowns. And if one of those is able to change history, well, you don't exist and you never did."

Chapter Thirty-Two

New York, New York
1913

Mary, Dalton, Diana, and Felix ate at the long table in Dalton's formal dining room. The conversation was muted after the discussions of the afternoon.

David rushed in right as they began to eat. "Sorry, Uncle, I had some errands in town. Oh, it's the man from the future. He's still here." David sat down.

"What did you do with the plane?" Felix asked. He still had bad memories of that night.

"We melted it down. It no longer exists."

Diana set her fork down. "Aren't you changing the future by being here and bringing children into the world?"

"Yes and no. I'll be in this house over a hundred years from now. I was invited by the general who will own it in the future, that night I found out that I would be stuck in time. The historian asked me if I had a rich ancestor because a man named Dalton built this house. Only, it wasn't my ancestor, it was me and I knew it. I know how the timeline works with my being here."

She picked up a fork and didn't say another word for a few minutes. Remembering her manners, she engaged in small talk the rest of the evening and didn't bring up time travel anymore.

Diana and Felix took the late train home. She had to work the early shift for breakfast. He walked her from the train station to her apartment and said goodnight there. He didn't go home right away but enjoyed the night air. In his time, neighborhoods like this one would have drug dealers and violence, but tonight it was peaceful and calm.

Despite being relaxed, he tossed and turned all night. At one point, he got out of bed and looked himself in the mirror. *Why can't I sleep? What's bothering me?* Then it dawned on him. *Dalton's sitting in the fancy mansion of his, dictating what I can and can't do.* He hatched a plan right there and then. *He doesn't control my future.*

In the morning he rushed down to the café. Diana was there waiting tables.

"What are you doing here? Your shift doesn't start until noon." she asked.

"We can do it. We can change history any way we want. We can stop wars. We can stop recessions. We'll do it together."

"I thought you said we couldn't mess with the timeline."

"Dalton won't mess with the timeline, but we can. If I get to the time machine before he does, I can hide it and send a message to the future to tell them to come get me, come get us. Then we change time, if it doesn't work, we change it back. We can do it over and over again until we get it perfect."

"Oh, it sounds wonderful!" she hugged him.

Her father's voice, from behind the bar, grunted. "Get back to work."

"Right away, Dad."

Felix started working early. Every time Diana would come into the back, they would plot and stew again.

"How do we get the money to bring the plane up from the bottom of the ocean?"

"We don't. I'll contact the guy who actually did it, but I'll have him do it now, not in 1925. If we can beat Dalton to the plane, we can keep him from destroying it."

"Yes!" Her smile was back.

It took him a while to locate Ted Hart. The man liked his privacy. Rich from listening to Dalton's stock picks, Ted had retired from the stock market to live in a New York penthouse. Security was tight and you would have to have a very good reason to talk to Ted. Only Ted decided if the reason was good enough.

Felix walked up to the front desk of the hotel. "I need to see Ted Hart." It had taken him several weeks to find out where the man lived. He was proud of his detective skills.

"I don't know who you're talking about." The man behind the desk turned to the next customer.

"But it's important."

"Sorry, Sir, you must have the wrong hotel."

He was sure of his research. Then it dawned on him. He slipped the man a twenty. "If a Ted Hart ever checks in here, please give him this message." He scrawled out a note on the hotel's stationery.

I am from the same time and place R. Adalwolf Dalton is. If you're interested in the machine of his, I can help you get it, and help you figure out how it works. Then Felix wrote down his address.

"Yes, Sir," the receptionist said. "If any Ted Hart checks in here, I'll make sure to get him this message." With a wink, the man stuffed it in his pocket.

Chapter Thirty-Three

New York, New York
1913

A loud knock shook Felix's door in the morning. He checked the time. It was six, and he rolled over and tried to ignore it. *Kids.*

Louder knocking forced him to get up. He jerked open the door only to see three large men in black suits looming over him. Their hats were pulled down so far over their eyes that Felix couldn't tell what color they were.

"You need to come with us. Get dressed."

"Who are you?"

The largest one walked into the room, pushing Felix out of the way. "You have five minutes."

Felix threw on some clothes, then walked back out. The tall one led the way while the other two stood on each side of him. After heading down the stairs and out the door, he was shoved into the back of a big green car with plush leather seats. The goons, as Felix thought of them, sat on either side while the large guy drove.

They arrived at the same hotel he had been a couple of days before. The elevator took them to the penthouse level. When the doors opened, the largest goon pushed Felix into the room. "Here he is, boss."

A man in a brown terrycloth bathroom, sporting short hair and a pipe looked Felix up and down. "I'm Ted. Tell me what you want."

"The time machine. I can help you find it."

"I don't know what you're talking about." Ted turned around and started to walk away.

"You will find it in 1925 without my help, but you can do it much sooner if you have my help."

Ted spun back around, "What year does World War I start?"

"Next year, but the United States doesn't enter the war until around 1918."

Checking his list, Ted replied, "It doesn't tell me when the United States enters, just it starts in 1914. When does World War II start?"

"I'm not a history buff, but I think it was 1938. I know the U. S. enters the war on December 7, 1941."

"The war starts in 1939, but close enough. Where is the time machine?"

"It's on the bottom of the ocean. I need you to save it before Dalton destroys it."

"Then you'll help me fix it so I can move back and forth through history?" Ted smiled.

"Yes, of course." Felix knew it would never happen, but if Ted knew that the machine would be worthless to him, he'd never agree to find it.

"Tell me how I find it and bring it up."

"You contact this salvage company," Felix wrote a note on a piece of paper. "They find it by watching ships go around an obstruction on the ocean floor."

"Hmm," Ted scratched his chin. "I'll have to pay them a visit."

Felix made it to work on time, despite the interruption in his life. When Diana brought back some dishes into the kitchen, he pulled her aside. "It's all set. I've talked to Ted. Soon we'll be rescued from this timeline and start going back in forth in time."

She clapped her hands for joy. "You did it. I'm so proud. Imagine, we can stop all wars before they start." She gave him a quick peck on the cheek.

Several weeks passed by before Felix heard from Ted. It was the banging on the door at six in the morning that roused him. He flung open the door, dressed this time. "Do we need to keep doing this?"

The large goon didn't even speak this time. He grunted. Pointing down the stairs.

Felix led the way this time. They climbed into the same car for the trip to the hotel. Ted was wearing the same bathrobe he had before. "There's a problem. The guy doesn't have a big enough crane to pick up whatever is down there."

"So, buy him a bigger crane. Imagine, going to your broker and knowing how much a stock is going to sell for in a few months. You would know what to buy and when to sell it without ever losing a dime. You'll be able to buy hundreds of cranes." The first step, in Felix's mind, was to get the machine off the sea floor. He'd figure out the details later.

Chapter Thirty-Four

New York, New York
1914

Winter snows and rough seas prevented any salvage operations until early May. Felix stayed working in the diner so he could be close to Diana. They would whisper plans back and forth to each other of how they would change the timeline to create a better world.

One morning early in June, a knock came on his door. It wasn't the jolt you out of bed knock that the goons did, but a normal knock. Felix pulled on the robe he had learned to put on the bed for these occasions. To his surprise, the goons were standing there.

"Today's the day," the big one said. After Felix was dressed, they headed down to the car and drove straight out to the docks.

Ted was there, smiling like a kid in a candy store. "We've located it. I thought you might want to be here when we raise it up."

Felix swallowed hard. He knew that Ted wouldn't be happy when he saw what state the time machine was in. "Oh," was all he could squeak out.

Boarding a tug boat, they sailed out to two barges. A large crane sat on the one. The tugboat tied up to the other barge.

A salty old sea captain came up to them. He had a faded, sweat-stained hat and a grey stubble of a beard. "She's down there, all right. It's large, too. Had to get a bigger crane. I've got divers lashing it to the crane hook. Should be done any moment now." The man smiled, showing his chewing tobacco stained teeth.

"Good, Felix here is going to fix it and then I'll be all set." Ted folded his arms. "Aren't you, Felix."

"May take a few months, depending on what shape she's in, but sure." He wasn't a good liar and seeing how Ted was giving him a sideways glance, he knew this time was no exception. He didn't know he'd be dragged out to the salvage operation. He had to figure out a different plan that didn't include trying to fix an irreparable time machine.

Divers were wrenched to the surface. Large helmets covered their head. It was bolted on to a suit and had airlines protruding out the back. All three of the men had someone helping them out of their equipment.

"She's ready." One of the men reported to the captain.

The captain shouted at the crane operator. "Bring her up."

Smoke billowed out of the steam engine as the lines grew taut. The machine struggled under the load. The barge began to tip dangerously to the one side.

"Stop." The captain rushed up the cab of the crane. "Stop!"

The lines went slack and the barge righted itself.

"It's too heavy. I'll need another barge."

In a quiet corner bar, in the back corner, sat Adalwolf Dalton and one of Ted's goons named Peter. Dalton scowled as he listened.

"They almost brought it up, but the thing was too heavy. It came close to taking the barge down. The captain is gonna need a bigger crane and larger barges. It'll take a couple of weeks before he's ready."

"Thank you." Dalton slipped him an envelope. "Keep me posted."

Peter smiled as he looked inside.

"Not here." Dalton snapped. "Wait until you're alone. Leave now so I can. We can't leave together."

"Yes, Sir." Peter rushed out the door.

Where does Ted get these idiots? Dalton stood up and made his way to the bar.

"Your usual, Mr. Dalton?"

"Yes."

"Coming right up." Dalton didn't have an office so he conducted all his business in the corner booth. The bartender never gave it a second thought of who Dalton was talking to. All he knew was, Dalton was good for business.

Dalton walked into the office of Smithfield Salvage company. The owner was tightening a bolt on a dive suit. "How can I help you?"

The equipment was all around, there was only a small space on the nearly buried desk for Dalton to set down a map. "How far is the continental slope from this spot?" He pointed to it on the map.

"About three miles. I've seen that spot before. A guy name, Tim, or Tom, wanted me to do some work there, but he got a cheaper bid from someone else."

"His name was Ted."

"Yep, that's it."

"You see, what's down there belongs to me, not Ted. I don't want him getting it."

"Ted has all the heavy equipment tied up. I guess what he took with him the first time wasn't large enough. I'd have to go to Boston to get the right equipment."

"The equipment he brought back will work just fine. I don't need to pick it up, I need it moved off the continental shelf."

"I see. I'm pretty pricey compared to those other guys."

"I know, that's why I'm here. I need the job done right."

Chapter Thirty-Five

New York, New York
1914

The same equipment Ted used was back over the wreck. Dalton stood on the deck of the barge as the crane lowered the chains.

Wilson stood next to him. "My divers have it all strapped up and we'll begin dragging it as soon as we have the chains hooked up."

"Has Ted found out we're here?" Dalton asked.

"Not yet. I rented the equipment he needs for the week. I had my guys take it out a mile and sit there. Ted and his guys are in Boston waiting for it to come back. They have no idea we're here."

"Good."

The chain went taut as the crane bellowed out smoke. "Got her. The dive boat will pick up my divers. We can start hauling."

With the barges strapped together, two large tugs pulled on them. The barges dipped down at a steep angle. A wide-eyed Dalton grabbed on to a post.

Wilson smiled. "No worries. I've calculated this all out. The barges won't tip over."

The angle of the deck decreased as the tugs picked up speed. "I do admit, I was a little worried."

Wilson smiled, "She's moving. It should be smooth sailing until we reach the shelf. We'll drop off your plane and then blow her to bits with the charges we set. I do have to say, it would have been cheaper for you to let me blow it in place."

"I want to make sure no one ever finds it. The future of mankind is at stake."

Wilson turned, "You're joking, right? I mean, this isn't that important, is it?"

Dalton nodded. "It is."

"Wow." Wilson watched the horizon. "Ted is going to be angry. Why did he want this thing, anyway?"

"He wanted to change the world to his advantage. Now he'll never be able to."

"I didn't like the guy, anyway." Wilson moved to the front of the barge. Looking down, he pulled one of the lines tighter on the timbers that held the barges together. "Not much longer and we'll be there. We're going to leave a trench where we pulled this along. One good storm will wash it all away. It's not every day you get to save the world."

Dalton didn't say anything. He didn't know if Wilson was baiting him or not. He had just met the man and couldn't size him up yet. An hour later, the tugs stopped. The crane had let out chain as the depth increased. It was now at the end of its spool.

"Here we are. My divers can't swim this deep so I'm going to let the chain go then back off when we set off the charges."

Dalton nodded. The end of the chain slipped into the water. Wilson and Dalton climbed aboard a tug. The timbers connecting the barges were loosened and the other tug took the two barges in tow.

Wilson held the plunger to the detonator. "Just say the word."

Dalton took a breath, "Now."

A column of water thirty feet high pushed up from the depths. Both Wilson and Dalton were drenched despite being back, away from the explosion. "Wow," Wilson brushed his face with his hand. "I didn't expect it to be that big."

Dalton sat there a moment. *I just blew up the remains of Captain Myers*. He knew he had to fix that. "It was impressive. Let's get out of here."

As they sailed back to New York, in the distance they could see a barge carrying a long crane. Wilson pointed it out to the captain of the barge, steer clear of that ship. I don't want them figuring out what we did."

The captain nodded and changed course. Back on dry land, Dalton drove home. Mary met him at the door. "Well, is it done?"

"Yes, blown to bits."

"No more planes landing in my backyard in the middle of the night?"

"No more."

"Good, now I can get some sleep and the children will stop having nightmares."

"We can only hope." He looked her in the eyes. "I need to do something for Myers. I blew up his remains. I need to leave at least a marker there."

"Where you blew up the plane?"

"No, I don't want to bring attention to that spot. I'll leave it where he was in one piece last. Where the plane rested for all those years. That's where I'll put it."

Chapter Thirty-Six

New York, New York
1914

"Just a cup of coffee, Ma'am."

Diana almost dropped the pot when she realized who it was. Instead of pouring the coffee, she ran back into the kitchen. "It's Dalton. He's here and he doesn't look happy."

Felix wiped his hands on a towel. Leaving his sink full of dishes, he walked out into the diner and sat down across from Dalton. "What do you want?"

"I'll start with some coffee."

Felix nodded for Diana to pour him a cup. She did, but stayed at the side of the booth, still holding the pot.

Dalton took a sip. "That was quite the stunt you pulled, showing Ted where to find the plane."

"It's too late for you to stop him. His equipment is already on site," Felix replied.

"And what are you going to do when he asks you to fix it?"

Felix shifted nervously in his seat. "I'll cross that bridge when I come to it. For now, I'm getting the plane. I can let the future know I'm here. They will come and rescue me."

Diana piped up, "We're going to end all wars and make the world safe."

Dalton stood up, put a dime on the table for the cup of coffee. "Idealist. You can't stop a war without creating three more. More suffering is what you accomplish, not less. You can destroy your very existence if you're not careful." He faced Felix. "You'll never be rescued. You have to realize that. Make a life in the here and now and live it." He walked out.

Diana turned to Felix. "Is he right? Will we just cause more problems?"

"I could destroy my very existence." He shivered. "I hadn't thought of that."

"What about all those that will die? I don't know what to do."

He turned to face her. "They died last time. They will die again."

Tears formed in her eyes. "It's so horrible."

Felix's door splintered open and Ted's goons barged into his apartment and dragged him out of bed. They didn't wait for him to get dressed, but forced him down the stairs in his pajamas and stuffed him into the awaiting black sedan.

"What's this all about?" Felix demanded.

"Shut up while you still can."

The car drove up to Ted's hotel. They dragged him through the door and sat him in a chair. They stood on either side of him.

Ted walked into the room. He pointed a gun at Felix. "I spent all this money to bring that time machine to the surface. Where is it?"

"It's there, just where I showed you it was. You saw it right?" Felix swallowed.

"It's not there anymore. Where did you take it?"

"Dalton." Felix stared straight ahead. "Dalton has it. He came to the diner to scare me off, but I didn't scare. I didn't tell him we had found it. He seemed to already know. He called me a fool. He has it, I'm sure he does."

"That girl of yours tell him?" Ted stood closer to Felix.

"No, she would never. She wants to end the World Wars. She wouldn't tell him. I want to get back to my time. Why would I tell him? He would destroy it, I'll be stuck. I have to go and see if I can get it back. It's so important. I'm the only one around, besides him, who can fly the thing."

"Go, then." Ted motioned with his gun.

The two men brought him back to his apartment. He grabbed some clothes then took the train over to Dalton's place.

It was a cold reception this time. He was led into the parlor without a word being spoken. He sat down and waited a while before Dalton made it downstairs.

"Please tell me where you took the Vmax3 drive. I need it intact."

Dalton sat down and smiled. "I dragged it away and then blew it to tiny bits. You'll never find it."

"I'm stuck!" Felix went pale.

"You always have been stuck. You don't have it so bad. The girl likes you. Settle down, raise a family. Enjoy your new life."

Felix stood up. "You have just ruined my life. I'm stuck here now." He stomped out and slammed the door behind him.

Chapter Thirty-Seven

Budapest Hungary
1914

Felix and Diana stood on the sidewalk. Felix found himself wishing he knew his history better. He didn't remember the man's name, but he knew it was during the ArchDuke's visit that the assassination would happen. He and Diana had eloped so her father would allow her to go with Felix on the trip. He was old fashioned. They would spend their honeymoon stopping the Great War.

The ArchDuke's motorcade was coming down the street. It was coming fast. The only thing Felix could do was yell, "Watch out. They are trying to kill you." He heard Diana screaming the same thing.

Policemen came up behind them. *"Šta radiš?"*

The ArchDuke's car made a wrong turn down an alley. As it backed out, two shots rang out. Mass pandemonium erupted, people running in all directions.

One of the officers grabbed Felix's arm and led him away. He looked over his shoulder to see Diana also being detained. They were both thrown into a cell at the police station and left there.

The holding cells were next to each other. A young man was put in with Felix also.

Felix turned to Diana. "We failed. All we have succeeded in doing is getting ourselves in trouble."

Hours passed by before someone came in to talk to them. It was a dour, pudgy man in an ill-fitting suit. He couldn't understand them, so he left. An hour later, he came back with a young, tall man who was very thin. They took Felix to an interview room.

"I am Huran. Um, I can talk to you. What is your name?"

"Why do you need my name? You have my passport."

Huran turned back to the other man, "*Pasoš*." The man handed the passports over to Huran. "I see, Americans. Yes, Mr. Felix Schmidt. Why did the Americans want the Arch Duke dead?"

"No, we tried to warn the ArchDuke of the murder plot. We tried to stop it."

"So, you deny that you are from America?"

"I'm from America, but America didn't want the Arch Duke dead."

"So, how do you know this? Did your government tell you this?"

Felix sat back in his chair, his heart racing. "I want a lawyer."

"Of course, you do, but that is not up to me." Huran leaned forward. "Were you part of the planning for this assassination?"

"No, I just barely got here."

"So, you came to make sure the deed was done right?"

"No, I came to warn him. I came to save his life."

"So, you admit you knew about the plot in advance? How else would you have known to warn him?"

"I'm not answering any more of your questions."

Huran turned to the large short man sitting behind him. They talked, but Felix couldn't understand a single thing they were saying. They both stood up. "You will see the judge in the morning."

Diana was brought into the same room that Felix had been in. Wide-eyed, she gazed around the room. It was no more than a square box with a table and some chairs. Huran and the pudgy man walked in and sat down.

"Please be seated, Mrs. Schmidt." Huran motioned to a chair.

Reluctantly, she sat down.

"Please tell us how you learned of the plot to kill the Arch Duke."

"I didn't know. Felix told me. I tried to stop it."

"I see, Felix has put you up to his scheme." He leaned back in his chair.

"Yes, we were going to stop the war."

Huran turned back to the other man and they talked for a minute, before turning back to Diana. "What war?"

"The Great War."

"No war is great. Who are the other conspirators?"

"I don't know."

"I see." Huran wrote down some notes. "Will you testify to the fact that Felix knew the Arch Duke was going to be assassinated?"

"Yes, if you want me to."

To Diana's surprise, they released her. She walked back to her hotel room. The military was out in force. Slipping past the desk clerk quietly, she made her way up to her room, then crumpled on the bed and sobbed.

Chapter Thirty-Eight

Budapest Hungary
1914

Felix stared up at the ceiling of his cell. It was dirty with cracking plaster, like the rest of his cell. A clank brought his attention to the metal door. It swung open. The guard grumbled and motioned him to come. He climbed off his cot and walked toward the man. Two more guards appeared and shackled Felix, then led him away.

The courthouse was full of people. They jeered Felix as the police led him through the room. One person took a swing at him, causing the police to push back the crowd. Right before they led Felix into the courtroom, the policemen took off his shackles. With two police officers on either side of him, they marched him into the room.

After the judge came in, Felix was sat down between two men at a table. One stood up right away and addressed the judge. Felix couldn't understand a word being spoken except he heard his name mentioned once in a while.

"You very lucky. You have a good lawyer," The man on his right whispered.

"What are they talking about?" He whispered back.

"Um, how do you say, um, deal. You are being sentenced, but only ten years, very lucky."

"What? I didn't plead guilty." Felix's voice was raised.

A rap on the bench by the judge's gavel drew Felix's attention. His lawyer sat down next to him. "Yes, you did plead guilty. I entered the plea for you. If I let you go free, the crowd would rip you to pieces. They want blood and yours would do as much as the real culprits."

"But, I didn't do anything wrong."

"It doesn't matter. You've already pled guilty. The United State's government and Mr. Dalton want you out of the limelight and into prison as quick as possible. They do not want to be implicated in the death of a foreign head of state in any way shape or form."

They all stood up as the judge did. He left to his chambers. Felix turned to his lawyer. "So, I'm a scapegoat?"

"No, you're a fool who should have minded his own business. I had no way of winning this case. My government and your government hired me to sweep this under the rug as quickly as possible. Your own wife was set to testify against you."

"My wife? Where is she?"

"On her way back to America." The lawyer walked out of the courtroom.

Outside, they shackled Felix up again, then marched him out of the courthouse. Again, people screamed at him. One lady threw a shoe. It hit one of the guards. The guard struck Felix on the back of the head. "This is all your fault. I should let the crowd kill you."

"Stop it," The other guard rebuked.

When they all arrived at the cell, Felix felt safe for the first time that afternoon. The bars kept him in, but it also kept those who hated him out. The quiet gave him time to reflect. *Ten years. I'm sentenced to prison for the next ten years. She's gone! On her way back to America. Your own wife was set to testify against you.* "Why did you abandon me Diana." He slumped down in the corner.

A loud knocking came on the front door. "Mr. Dalton, Mr. Dalton. They have Felix, Mr. Dalton."

Mary answered it. "Come in, you poor dear. What are you going on about?"

"The Austrians took Felix. Mr. Dalton has to come and help."

Mary led Diana into the parlor. "I'll go get Adalwolf."

"I'm here." Dalton walked into the parlor from the study.

"They took Felix."

"I know. He's been sentenced to ten years. There's nothing I can do."

"But he didn't do anything."

Mary brought in some tea. "Sit, I just made a pot. This will calm your nerves."

Diana sat down and balanced the teacup on her lap. "You must help, Mr. Dalton."

Dalton sat down and leaned back, crossing his legs. "I did help. I told you not to go. You didn't listen."

"But what can we do now?" Her eyes filled with tears.

"Nothing. It's the timeline correcting itself. Felix was a blip, and now he's gone. His chances of surviving ten years in an Austrian prison are not good."

"Adalwolf, don't be so heartless." Mary scolded. She patted Diana's hand. "There, there."

"Heartless? They almost ruined the timeline and threatened my very existence. She was set to testify against Felix at the trial."

"I was not!" Diana's face reddened.

"You didn't read the papers, did you? We're you going to say that Felix knew that the Arch Duke would be assassinated?"

"Yes, because he did."

"That makes him a conspirator. Only the conspirators knew of the assassination beforehand."

She gasped and put her hand over her mouth. "I didn't think…"

"With your testimony, the prosecution had an airtight case. They would have hanged him. I did do something. I hired the most expensive lawyer in Austria. I got him off with only ten years in prison. If he can survive that, you'll see him again."

Chapter Thirty-Nine

Budapest Hungary
1920

Diana went back to work in her father's café. She wrote Felix weekly, but never knew if her letters were getting through. There was no response from him.

One day, after the war, she determined to see him. She knocked on Dalton's door in the early afternoon.

Felix, for his part, was miserable. The food was bad and the sanitation non-existent. He was often sick. Still, he knew he was much better off than the poor men in the trenches.

Princip died in prison. He was the man who shot the Archduke, thus starting the war. Felix had met him, but avoided him afterward because Princip had tuberculosis. As the war raged on, the conditions in the prison deteriorated. Food became scarce and most of the competent guards were sent to the front. The ones left were scoundrels in Felix's mind, pitting prisoners against each other. Most of them would have been incarcerated themselves, if not for the war.

By the end of the war, Felix had lost half his body weight. He was sick more than he was healthy. He mostly sat in the corner of his cell staring into space. One day, a guard opened the cell door and threw in some clothes. "Get dressed," he said.

A few minutes later, the guard led him out of the cell and to the front gate. "You are free to go." The gate closed behind him. He tried to see, but his eyes weren't accustomed to the bright noonday sun.

"Felix," a voice rang out.

"Diana, is that you?" He squinted to see three people coming towards him.

"Don't touch him, Diana, at least until we get him cleaned up and deloused," Dalton urged.

Diana stopped in her tracks. A car pulled up.

"Felix, this cab will take you to the doctor, where you will be checked over and cleaned up. Then we'll meet up with you," Dalton said.

Felix shrugged and got into the car. At least he was still alive.

At the office, they stripped him naked, weighed him, sprayed him with some chemical, shaved his head, and then showered him. He was dressed in a nice suit and tie, then pushed out of the office.

Dalton, Mary, and Diana were waiting for him when he left the office.

Diana hugged him. He couldn't remember when a hug felt so good. He then turned to Dalton. "They shaved my head."

"You had lice. It's the easiest way to get rid of it." He put a bowler hat on Felix's head. "It will grow back, meanwhile, wear the hat."

Adjusting the hat, Felix asked, "How did you get me out?"

"Most of the conspirators in the death of the Archduke were having their sentences commuted, so I asked my lawyer to see what he could do for you. He was able to get your sentence commuted too."

"Thank you so much. What is to become of me now?"

"You are extremely malnourished, according to the doctor's report. I am to fatten you up, but that will have to wait. We need to get back as soon as possible. Here, the United States Government has issued you new identification papers because they want no notoriety about you coming back home. You are now Jakob Franz, while you are traveling, at least. We'll get you back to the states and go from there."

Dalton handed him the papers. He looked over them. "Thank you again. When do we leave?"

"Right now."

Another cab pulled up a few minutes later and the group climbed in. They were dropped off at the train station.

Steam and smoke billowed out of the train as it made its way to the coast. Felix sat across from Dalton. "Thanks again for helping me."

"Are you done with this nonsense then? World War One is over, are you going to try and stop the next war? It's coming in a few short years."

'I'm done."

Dalton sat back. "Good."

The next day they boarded a ship heading towards America. Felix had night tremors. Diana held him. As he lay in her arms, he asked, "What will become of me, of us? I know too much."

"You will work for Dalton. It's all set. Those things he doesn't remember of the future, you will fill him in on. He's adapted to the circumstances well, you will also."

Felix nodded. "I'm ready to accept my fate. It's a lot better fate than it was just a few days ago."

Chapter Forty

Long Island, New York
1920

Felix stood on the deck of the ship during its voyage. He couldn't sleep. The nightmares had started and it jolted him awake every time he drifted off. He stared out across the empty sea. He felt gentle arms around his waist.

"Come back to bed. I'm lonely," Diana put her cheek against his.

"It's so good to be free, but my mind isn't. I've seen murders, suffering, and brutality. My mind isn't letting go."

"Okay, we can just sit here arm in arm and watch the waves go by then."

He nodded, "I would like that."

It was the first week back in the United States. Dalton had opened up an office on Long Island, halfway between New York and the Hamptons. Diana wanted to be near her father. He had taken a turn for the worse while Felix had been away, so the two of them stayed in the city. Diana did most of the cooking in the diner these days. Her father helped where he could.

Felix walked into the office, a one-story building next to the main road. The land would be worth a fortune in only a few years. He sat down at his desk. An old typewriter greeted him. Dalton walked in a few minutes later.

Felix looked up, "What am I supposed to be doing?"

"Good morning," Dalton smiled. "I need to know a few things to fill in the blanks of history." He walked in the office and then came back out with a list of questions. "Here, fill in the answers for me. You can use the typewriter or you can just write down the answers." Dalton walked back into his office.

Felix looked at the first one. "How did they come to get their hands on the Vmax3 drive?"

He put a piece of paper in the typewriter and pushed a key. Nothing happened. He pushed it harder. Still nothing. He slammed it down. It finally left a mark. "How do you use this contraption?" he yelled through the door.

"It takes a lot of getting used to, especially if you've just come off of using a computer keyboard. Write down the answers."

Felix sighed, then pulled out a pen. *Fountain pen.* He sighed again. He hadn't needed to write anything down while a prisoner, or a dishwasher. Diana had done that for him, those few times he needed it. "Is the pencil invented yet?"

Dalton came in the room. "Here, sorry I forgot all the troubles I had adjusting to this time." He put two pencils on the desk and walked back to the office.

Felix pulled the paper out of the typewriter and set it on the desk. Pushing the typewriter aside he wrote.

There are several copies of the Vmax3 drive in existence in my century. Phillip Anderson was sent back in time to bring you back, so you could explain what went wrong. He never made it back to our time. The plane was found in the 1970s with holes in the oil tank. No word on Anderson's fate ever surfaced.

It is suspected that a pirated copy of the Vmax3 drive made it away from the Lockheed plant, but was never proven. Phillip Anderson did smuggle a copy of the plans for the plane out of Boeing, but that would mean nothing without the Vmax3 drive. If the same people have a copy of the drive and the plane, it would still require a massive amount of money to develop it and the expertise to build it. So far as I know, nobody has tried. If a foreign government has both of those, then the past and the future is theirs.

Two completed planes existed. The FBI had one but it was destroyed by the CIA. The government agencies didn't trust each other. You destroyed the other. I left a man in the seventies to destroy the one that Phillip Anderson flew. I have no idea if he succeeded.

Senator James has been, or I should say, will be, sent to prison for his role in procuring the money for the plane. The timeline will be very different now that your copy is destroyed. I will not be coming back in that version of history.

Dalton's next question was, "What would the future be like if Ted would have found the plane?"

Ted brought the plane up from the depths, but it was in rough shape. It was 1925 before he did though, so that's in the future. If I hadn't interfered, that is. He tried for years to get it to work, but then gave up and visited you. Because you were dying of prostate cancer, he thought you would jump at the chance to fix it and go back to get treated. He never made it home, but died in a car crash.

Ted's son Mel tried to fix the plane also, but Bryan found out and received a court order to take the plane. Mel murdered him and went to prison. The plane bounced around until it ended up in Senator James' hands. He was able to rebuild the plane and the Vamx3 drive. That was the plane Phillip Anderson flew back to you and ended up in the seventies.

How can we stop these visits back to the 1900s?

I think you did already.

Dalton came back into the room and read over the answers. He swallowed. "This is hard to read." He walked out without saying another word.

Felix ventured into Dalton's office, after knocking on the door. Dalton looked up. "I've already messed the time line up, so it's irreparable. I've done the same thing you spent five years in prison over. I'll still die, but my son won't. What happens if he has kids? I don't know what to do. I thought I could stop Hitler, one little boy drowns, history heals itself. It doesn't work. Every child has an impact. What am I going to do?"

Felix looked at him long and hard. "I thought it was so easy for you. I never realized. You watch the *Titanic* go down and couldn't lift a finger. You let me rot in prison. I'm not bitter. You did what you thought was right, but here we are still, messing with our own future. The future me will not come back in time. I've changed the timeline by being here. We may have ruined our own lives."

Dalton took a deep breath. "Worse than that, I thought my nephew was on the ship and I still let it go down." He went over and pulled up a chair. "We will do the best we can not to mess up the timeline. That's all we can do."

Felix nodded. "Agreed."

Chapter Forty-One

New York, New York
1919

Dalton walked into the yard of the stonemason. All around him, men chiseled away on stones. A few had lean-to shelters, but most of them were exposed to the elements. A short man with a leather apron on came up to Dalton.

"How can I help ya, Sir?"

"I need a stone cut."

"How big a stone?"

"I want a large cross, about my height, made of granite. I want this inscription on it." Dalton handed him a folded piece of paper.

"Just a second." The man whistled and a boy of about fourteen came up. "My eyes aren't so good for reading small stuff. Read it to me, Paul."

"Yes, Sir." Paul unfolded the paper. "Says, Captain Gerald Myers. Born September 15, 2012. Died January 6, 1894."

The short man hit Paul upside the head. "Read it right."

"That's what it says, Pa."

The man turned to Dalton. "I think there's a mistake, Sir. Did you mean September 15, 1812?"

"No, I meant 2012. That's how I want the stone inscribed. I have a reason for doing it that way."

The man shrugged, "It's your money. I need some cash up front to buy that much granite."

Dalton nodded, "Of course."

Dalton picked up the Cross three weeks later. The tug chugged out into the Atlantic Ocean. It pulled a barge with a small crane on it. The cross was wrapped in tarps and tied securely on the deck. The tug stopped and anchored. The captain walked out of the pilot house. "This is the spot. I'll send my divers down first. They will secure the cross as we lower it."

Dalton, Felix, Mary, David, and Bryan stood on the deck of the tug, watching the divers descend. Later, a yank on the line indicated the divers were in place. The crane puffed smoke and the cross was attached to it. Pulling it up and slowly dropping it down, the crane let out line.

Another yank, the crane took in line and the divers came up.

Dalton cleared his throat. "None of you knew Captain Myers, but he was a good man. He deserved a lot more than to die so far away from home and so far out of his time. He could be irritating at times, but he died doing his duty like the good soldier that he was."

Dalton nodded to the captain and the ship pulled anchor and headed back to the city.

At the office the next morning, Dalton was late. Felix finished up on some of the assignments he'd been given. When Dalton came in, he turned to Felix and said, "You need to get away from the East Coast. Move to Alaska. I've told my son not to have kids, but he just laughed at me. I don't know what to do. I'm going to destroy history."

"It's cold in Alaska."

"Not so bad, if you're on the coast. Nobody history-changing ever came out of Alaska."

Felix shook his head. "You're overreacting. Most people are born, grow up, and then die and don't make a dent on history. We're going to be okay. You are talking about killing Hitler. He was a major player in history. What about that sugar beet farmer in Idaho? How does his life and death impact history?"

Dalton sat down. "I don't know. I just don't know."

"What's gotten you so upset?"

"We're going to destroy the timeline. I didn't know my son would die in this current timeline. Now his life, his very existence, changes everything. What if one of his kids, or your children, turn out to be evil?"

"What if they turn out good? What if they save mankind from a major disaster? That's just as likely. We have a right to live out our lives. We have been put in these circumstances beyond our control. History will have to adjust to us like it has to every single person that comes along."

Dalton smiled. "I've never heard you so profound." He stroked his chin. "You know, you're right. I should not have married. I should not have built up a fortune. I should have let Phillip take me back to my time, but yet, here I am. I'm going to live my life. I am going to do one more thing. I'm going to try and stop the time machine from being built. It's caused a lot of deaths."

Felix's eyes widened. "How is that going to affect history?"

"It will make sure I don't kill Hitler. If I fail to save him the next time around, it destroys the world. That bullet could have hit me as easily as it hit Myers."

"But you won't go back in time. You won't meet Mary."

"Perhaps you're right. I won't be alive to stop it anyway. I would have to send Bryan. I'm going to close down operations here. Your father-in-law is ailing, I heard. I can purchase the family diner and you can run it."

Felix smiled. "I see what you're doing. A small-time diner owner won't impact history. I would say no, but Diana would love it, so, yes."

Dalton nodded and left the room.

Chapter Forty-Two

The Hamptons, New York
1921

"You invented Chicken Fried steak?" Dalton, Mary, Felix, and Diana sat at the table in the newly remodeled diner.

"It was invented in Texas, but I was the first one to bring it to New York City." Felix smiled.

"It is very good," Mary commented, "I've never had anything like it."

"In our time, it's in nearly every good restaurant on the planet. Great idea, Felix, bringing it to New York. You two are doing good things here. The place looks great."

"Yes, it's the heyday of diners. In a decade or two, they will start to dwindle out, but I'll be retired by then."

"You two always talk in riddles," Diana replied. "It's so unnerving to know all that you do. What disaster is awaiting us next?" She shivered.

"Nothing much. This era will be referred to as the Roaring Twenties."

"When do I need to get out of the stock market?" Felix asked.

"What, he needs to get out of the stock market?" Diana eyed both men. "He's doing so well in it."

"Before 1929. It will lose almost half its value over a single week, but before then, you'll make lots of money." Dalton smiled. "No, you have nothing to worry about for years."

"Good," Diana replied.

"I heard Bryan is engaged," Felix commented.

"I tried to talk him out of it, but he wouldn't talk. He says he loves the girl." Dalton took another forkful.

"You shouldn't have tried. Honestly, he has a right to a full and happy life." Mary scowled at him.

"Well, dinner was delicious. Thank you so much." Dalton stood up and offered Mary his arm. "Should we head back home, Mrs. Dalton?"

She smiled and took his arm. "Yes, Mr. Dalton."

Felix looked around. "I love this place and time. I'm glad I came back. If I hadn't, I would never have met you."

She hugged him. "If only we could have had kids."

"Prison destroyed any chance of that. Besides, us having kids? That would have really worry Dalton."

Ted watched as Charles ran into his office. He was out of breath when he stood in front of Ted's desk. "They met again, at the diner. I couldn't get close enough to everything they said, but I overheard Dalton say something about the stock market losing its value."

"That must be the crash in 1929. Did they mention the time machine at all?"

Charles shook his head. "I think they destroyed it."

"I still want to hear everything they say to each other. Two men from the future will always talk about it."

"Yes, Sir."

Ted couldn't stand it anymore. The only way to get the information he needed was to talk to Dalton himself.

He didn't set an appointment, but drove to the house.

"Hello, Ted," Mary smiled. "What brings you all the way out here?"

"I need to talk to Adalwolf. Is he here?"

"Yes, of course, come in."

He walked into the parlor and Mary ran upstairs to get Dalton.

"Ted, good to see you, have a seat."

When he was settled, Ted said, "You beat me. I congratulate you."

"You couldn't have used the time machine anyway. It was badly decayed and the parts to fix it haven't been invented yet."

"Yes, but there's another one, isn't there?"

"Two more, as far as I know. I truly hope there aren't any others."

"What happened to those two?"

"One I destroyed and the other was stuck in the 1970s. I shot it full of holes. I hadn't expected that one. The second one I anticipated."

"They keep trying to take you back to the future. Why don't you go with them?" Ted leaned back in his chair.

"My life is here. The machine destroys time. I don't want any part of that. If they keep sending the new machines, I'll keep destroying them."

"Could you keep one of them? Let us see the future now and then to improve our portfolios?"

Dalton laughed. "I don't know if they will send any more, but no, I fear what the machines can do so I'll keep destroying them."

"Can't blame a guy for trying."

"Nope."

Ted stood up to leave, but shook Dalton's hand first.

He walked out of the house but didn't get into his car. Instead he had a meeting with a real estate agent who was waiting for him across the street.

"This is the property you asked about, Ted. What do you think?"

"I'll take it."

Chapter Forty-Three

Hamptons, New York
1946

Brian, and his son, Jacob, sat in the parlor of Adalwolf Dalton's home. They chatted as they waited for Grampa Wolf to come down. Soon the sound of slow footsteps coming down the stairs could be heard. Grampa Wolf turned the corner and slumped down in the nearest chair.

"This growing old isn't for the faint of heart."

"How are you doing, Dad?" Brian asked.

"Not bad, for an old guy."

"How old are you, now?" Jacob asked.

"That's a hard question to answer. Let's see, I was in my thirties in 1894, let makes me around eighty-six. If you consider I was born next century, I'm a whole lot of negative years old. I think my body feels around 68, so we're going with that."

Both father and son smiled.

"The reason I called you here," Dalton went on, "is that Felix tells me that I'll be dead of prostate cancer within the year. I need you two to find John Buck or Jason Ralston. He lives in the sixties in a small Arizona town. He holds the key to stopping the time machine, before it starts. If you can, talk him out of doing the time capsule and going back to his commander to tell him he traveled back in time. I need you two to stop him."

"Of course, Grampa, anything for you."

Brian nodded. "We will make sure and do that."

Dalton smiled. "Good. Poor Ted, moved next door in the vain hope of capturing a time machine. He must have thought we had one a month landing here."

"At least he has great barbecues during the summertime," Brian teased.

"Yes, he has great barbeques. In another timeline, his son, Mel, murders you, according to Felix," Dalton commented.

"He has always been a friend," Brian replied.

"The idea of controlling time is toxic. Anyway, I'm off to see Felix. Anyone wish to join me?"

Brian shook his head. "I love the food, but we have to visit his other grandfather today."

"All right, I'll see you two when you come back around."

Felix waited for Dalton to arrive. He paced back and forth. When Dalton finally stepped through the door, he said, "I saw a couple that looked out of place."

"What do you mean, out of place?'" Dalton asked.

"Like they were from the future, but didn't get the clothes quite right. They wore fifties clothes. The dress the lady had on wasn't from the twenties."

Dalton stroked his chin. "Do you think they were trendsetters?"

"No. They came in and ordered, but didn't identify themselves as from the future. They scanned the diner a lot. I think they were looking for you."

"Point them out if you see them again."

"I will."

"Meanwhile, how is Diana?"

Felix shook his head. "Not well. I thought I would go first after spending all those years in prison with bad food and disease constantly around me. They don't give her but a few weeks. If I could take her back, the doctors could cure her. It's a highly treatable form of cancer in our time."

"Were you hoping those people you saw were from the future so you could take her back and get her fixed up?"

Felix hung his head. "Yes, I was wishing that."

"It's a hard thing to accept, but we are doing the best we can for mankind. I'll die of prostate cancer before the year is out, too. We sacrifice so others can live their lives."

"I'd still take her to the future in a heartbeat so I could keep her."

"Can I see her?"

"She's upstairs."

A few moments later they both stood over her bed. She was thin and frail. Her eyes sunken in. Still she managed a smile. "Adalwolf, it's good to see you."

"How do you feel?"

"Like I've been hit by a runaway train."

"I wish you'd let me take you to the hospital," Felix interjected.

"I don't want to die in a hospital. I want to be here, in my home. I don't want to go to the future to be cured. I've lived my life. The doctors can't do a thing for me. I'll pass away soon."

Dalton patted her arm. "You're really brave."

She nodded, and opened her mouth to talk, but started coughing violently. Blood trickled out of her nose when she stopped. She quickly wiped it away.

"I'll leave you alone so you can rest."

When they were back downstairs, Felix replied, "It's almost too late. I've got to get her to the future soon."

Dalton shook his head slowly, "It is too late. Even if you were able to get her back, she's too far gone."

Felix slumped down in one of the diner's stools. "I know, but I hate to give up. I love her."

"I'm so sorry." Dalton patted his shoulder.

Chapter Forty-Four

New York, New York
1946

The clouds were threatening rain as the hearse pulled up. The grave was dug. Both Felix and Dalton were among the pallbearers. They pulled the casket out of the back and set it down on top of the supports over the grave.

The priest, Bible in hand, stepped forward. He read a few passages to the group gathered around. Sprinkling ashes, he said a few more words.

A man and woman appeared on the fringe of the congregation. Felix spotted them first. He nudged Dalton. "Those are the ones I told you about," he whispered.

Looking up, Dalton shrugged. "They could be anyone."

"They're looking at you. Why wouldn't they be looking at me, too?"

Dalton ignored him and went back listening to the priest. When the graveside service was over, he took Mary by the hand and headed to his car.

Felix walked towards the couple, but they walked off before he was able to catch them.

The next day at the diner, he let the assistant cook take over while he went to the library.

A knock came on Dalton's door, loud and persistent. Brian answered. "Hello, Felix, how can I help you?"

"Where is he?" Felix pushed past him.

"If you're talking about my father, he's on the back patio."

Felix stomped out there. Facing him, he yelled, "You killed me off. Imagine finding the headline, *American Dies in Austrian Prison*. I even found my obituary."

Dalton looked up from his paper. "I had to. You're weak. If they come for you, you will go."

"I could have saved her, if not for you."

Dalton shook his head. "It was her idea. She didn't want to live in the future. She wanted you to stay with her in the here and now. She asked me to do it. She died because she lived in the 1940s and they don't have the medication to save her."

"That couple that followed you, they were from the future, weren't they? They weren't looking for me because I'm dead, right. They talked to you after the funeral, didn't they?"

"No. No one talked to me after the funeral. I don't know who they were. I think you wanted them to be something they weren't. You are so desperate to get back to your own time, you're imagining time travelers all over the place."

Felix kicked the patio post, and stomped out.

"What was that all about?" Mary asked. She had brought out a tea server when she'd seen Felix out back.

"He just found out he died. He wasn't happy about it."

"Oh, that. Goodness, poor man. I was hoping he'd never figure it out. Do you think he'll ever be back?"

"Maybe, when he settles down."

Brian Dalton brought the group to the basement of his father's home in the Hamptons. They consisted of Brian, his wife, Gina, their son, Jacob, Mary's brother, David, and George and Betty Trumball.

They gathered around a wood replica of the Vmax3 time machine.

"This is it," Brian said. "I had David's help in recreating it as best as I could. Besides my father, mother, and Felix, we are the only ones that have seen it."

The plane stood ten inches off the ground and was two feet nose to tail with the wings around the same. Olive drab paint finished it out.

"It's so ugly," Betty commented.

"Yes, and it does ugly things too," Brian replied. "That is why we must stop it. Father has given me the task, I have asked all of you for help. George, here is keeping an eye on Felix. How is that going?"

"Not well. He's spotted us at the diner and again at the funeral. He thinks we're from the future. I heard he even talked to Adalwolf about us. We pretended to ignore him and look like we were trying to get a hold of Adalwolf, but that only increased his suspicion. He found out about his obituary around that time."

"We need to send someone else to do spy on him then. The only one of us he doesn't know is my son, Jacob."

All eyes turned to the young man. "I heard about the confrontation between Felix and my grandfather. I'll find an apartment across the street from the diner. I can keep tabs on him that way without being seen."

"Good idea," David nodded.

"Are we ready?" Brian asked.

Everyone nodded. Brian set the model on fire and they all joined hands around it. Brian began the chanting. "We pledge our lives to stop the time machine."

Chapter Forty-Five

The Hamptons, New York
1948

"I shouldn't be here." Felix stood at yet another graveside. "The last time I talked to Adalwolf, I yelled at him and kicked his house."

"Nonsense," Brian assured him. "You and my father shared a knowledge of the future. You were the only ones there. He liked you. I'm glad you came."

The service was over. A few people still milled around the casket. Dalton had finally succumbed to the prostate cancer after fighting a good fight. Mary, comforted by her grandchildren, made her way back to the car.

"He kept telling me to live where I am. I so wanted to go back, that I didn't take his advice."

"He adapted well, passing up on two opportunities to go back. You should try also."

"I stand no chance of getting rescued now. Diana saw to that. She wrote my obituary. The future thinks I'm dead. I thought I saw a couple from the future, but it turned out they weren't. Wishful thinking, I guess."

Brian patted him on the shoulder. "It's okay. You have your diner. You should be all set."

"I'm going to sell it. I want to travel. All the people around me are dying. I want to see the country before I go."

"Good idea. The car's waiting for me. I have to go. Enjoy the rest of your life in this century. These are the golden years of American prosperity."

"Yes, I think you're right."

The two shook hands and parted ways.

"What did that man have to say?" Mary frowned as Brian climbed into the car.

"He feels bad for yelling at Dad the last time they talked."

"He should. He would have gone back, if given the opportunity."

Brian smiled. "I'll make sure he doesn't come back in time so we won't have to worry about what he does or doesn't do."

She patted him on the knee. "Yes, you stopped all those fools. All except for my Adalwolf. Don't stop him. I had such a good life with that man. I was at a dead-end job when I met him. My brother called me an old maid. Papa didn't like him, but he came around."

"Yes, Mom. We'll stop all but one."

Felix stood in the field in Washington state. Above him, a new motor hotel was being built. *Ethan, if I live another thirty years, I'll stop you and me from getting trapped in the past.* He shuddered at the thought. *I was so cocky back then. Until I met Robert Adalwolf Dalton. He ruined my life. I intend to get it back.*

He walked up the hill. The construction manager came up to him. "This is the strangest hotel I've ever seen. There is no second floor and the rooms are spaced out so far."

"It's a motor hotel. The parking lot will face all the rooms. The idea is they can have their car in front of their room. I call it a motel, though. They are just starting to come into vogue. You'll see, there are lots of them going up all over the country."

"I hope you're right. Otherwise you've spent all this money for nothing."

"I'm right. I'm really good at reading the future. I made a quiet fortune doing that. My buddy wanted me to run my diner and live in obscurity, but I quietly invested money on the side while he wasn't looking. I'm rich now and am going to enjoy it, and why not? I knew what I needed to invest in."

The manager spit out a wad of chaw. "I'll get back to work then. As long as you know what you're doing."

Felix looked over the hillside. He was just far enough back not to scare the plane away from landing, but close enough to hear it when it did. He would then have a ride back to the life he left. Now that Diana was gone, he had no reason to stay here. It didn't matter, he would talk the younger version of himself into going back for her. Dalton wouldn't get the chance of destroying the time machine this time. It would take another thirty years, but he would save the machine and himself.

Chapter Forty-Six

Arizona
1966

John Buck sat eating a burger in front of the McDonald's. Lt. Granger came up and sat down. The two of them had a long conversation. When Granger left, John started to get up, but two men stopped him.

"Sit back down, Jason," the taller man said.

"His name is John Buck at this time," the other corrected.

"Is that my real name, Jason? Are you guys from the future coming to take me back?"

"Just sit down," the taller one commanded.

Jason did as he requested.

"I'm Jacob Dalton, and my tall friend here is Paul Trumball. We mean you no harm."

"What's going on?" John asked nervously.

Jacob leaned back in his chair. "We're from the past. A past we want to keep intact. We need your help doing that. Live your life exactly as you are, only don't put anything in a time capsule, and when you get older, don't visit your old commander. We need to stop a tragic event only you can help us."

John stared at them wide eye. "What event?"

"That's all we are at liberty to say."

"Of course, I do want to prevent a tragedy. How are you from the past and know about the future? How does that work? If you know about me, then what's my name and do I end up getting back to my time?"

Jacob leaned forward. "If I tell you any of that, it will destroy your future. All I'm asking you to do is not destroy our past." Both men stood up and walked away from the table.

John shrugged, but then went back to work.

When they were out of earshot, Paul turned to Jacob, "Do you think it will work?"

"No, we weren't forceful enough. What's our next option, if that one doesn't work?" Jacob replied.

Paul took a handwritten notebook out. Most of the pages were loose and some of them almost fell out when he opened it. Flipping through it, he said, Adalwolf believed the time capsule would be put in the ground in this week. If that doesn't happen, we're home free."

"Unless they skip that step. We need to have someone on the base, if Jason wants to talk to his old commander. We'll stop him before he steps into the office."

Looking over everything, Paul replied, "That's over forty-five years from now. We need to make sure we get this one because neither one of us might be alive at that point."

"You're a good-looking man. Figure out where the nurses hang out and flirt with one. If we have someone on the inside of the base, then we're in good shape. They can monitor Jason for us."

"You mean, John."

"John, that's right."

Susan, the nurse that had taken John in, picked him up at the hardware store. They were going clothes shopping.

"Hi," he said. "Thanks for doing this."

"Sure, John."

"Some guys who said they were from the past visited me today. One of them called me Jason."

"Is that your name? Does it ring a bell?"

"I don't know. I think they found out I have amnesia and were taking advantage of it. I'm going to ignore them."

"Sounds like a good plan." She started up the jeep and drove towards the clothing store.

On a barstool around the corner from the base, sat Mary, a petite redhead with a short dress on. Paul set down next to her and ordered a beer.

She turned and smiled, "Well, hello, there."

"Oh, hi." He sipped his beer.

She held out her hand, "I'm Mary, but the guys around here just call me 'Easy.'"

He snorted, "And you're okay with that?"

"No, I hate it. Just because I don't like being alone on a weekend, doesn't mean I'm easy. What's your name?"

"I'm Paul." He shook her hand.

"Glad to meet you, Paul. Are you a soldier at the base?"

"No, I am a traveler. My job is to investigate strange happenings. Do you work at the base?"

"Yes, I'm a nurse."

"Oh, did you hear about the plane crash near here? I heard they brought the survivors to your hospital."

"Survivor. There was only one. I didn't hear much about it. He has amnesia and was taken in by another nurse. I did hear the plane was interesting, but it's in pieces. I don't know much other than that."

"Well, Mary, what do you say that I get you out of this place and buy you dinner?"

She hopped off the bar stool, put a couple of dollars next to her unfinished drink. "Now we're talking."

Chapter Forty-Seven

Arizona
1966

Paul met Mary at the bar on a Friday night. She looked a little sheepish when she came in.

"What's wrong?"

"The time capsule, they built it. I hope you're not too upset."

He sat down on a bar stool. "Oh, no." His heart raced. "We talked to him about it. He didn't listen."

"It means forty-five years from now we'll have to try again."

Her eyes widened. "How do you know that?"

"Oh, oops. Crystal ball. I can see the future."

She put her hands on her hips, "Yeah, right."

He laughed, "Yep, I can see the future, I can see you going out to dinner with me again tonight."

Smiling, she said, "I'll give you that one. Where are we going?"

"That diner you like so much."

"Hmm, well, okay." She flashed him a smile.

"I have to make a phone call first; then I'll be right with you."

Paul dialed up Jacob. "John did it. He had them build the time capsule."

"Nothing we can do now, unless we can destroy it. Being in the middle of a military base, I don't think that will happen. We'll meet up with John Buck again. This time we'll be more forceful."

"Got it, but not tonight. I have plans."

Jacob and Paul sat on a hillside overlooking the town. Paul aimed the sniper rifle, crosshairs on John Buck's head. He hesitated. Taking a deep breath, he aimed again. Setting the rifle down, he said, "I can't do it. I'm not a murderer."

"It's for the greater good. We pledged our lives to destroy the time machine from history."

"*You* pledged *your* life. I wasn't there at the burning of the mock Vmax3 plane. I'm just carrying on for my father after he got sick."

"Give me that." Jacob grabbed the rifle. The older man didn't hold it as steady.

"Are we destroying the future, which destroys the present? If we kill him are you rewriting history and eliminating your entire family from existence? Everyone you loved will be gone."

Jacob set down the rifle. "I don't know. You're right, we shouldn't do this, but we have to do something."

"Your grandfather destroyed the time machine, maybe that's enough."

"Maybe." He thought for a minute. "You could be right. Let's get out of here before someone sees us."

As they drove down the hill, Jacob confessed, "I've asked Mary to be my wife."

Jacob turned to him and smiled. "You know the dangers of red-headed children."

Chuckling, Paul said, "Yep, going to name our first kid Peter."

"Oh, I get it, Peter, Paul, and Mary." He laughed. "Tell me you're not going to raise your kids in this rattlesnake-infested part of the world."

"No, she's from Philly, just stationed here. Her service is up in May. We'll marry in June, in New York. I'm going to take her back to where our families are."

"Hmm," Jacob scratched his chin. "We need to enlist her help. New York is the hub of activity when they design the Vmax3 plane. If your child could help us stop it, that would be great."

"She's going to think I'm an idiot and run away."

"We'll wait until after the wedding then. Break it to her slowly, a piece at a time."

"We have forty-five years."

Two and a half years after the marriage, Mary cleaned out one of the drawers and found Adalwolf's notebook. She sat down at the dining room table and began to read, her heart raced as she did. When Paul came into the room, she confronted him, "What is this?"

He sat down across from her. "I've been meaning to tell you about that. It's a long story. do you have the time?"

"What, yes of course."

"In the future, they invent a time machine. The first mission goes back to kill Hitler. It goes horribly wrong, and one of the men on the mission is killed, the other one is stuck in the past. John Buck is one of those who's stuck in the past, too."

"I heard rumors about that."

"Anyway, Jacob's grandfather hired my father and mother to help to stop the time machine from being built.

That is what they dedicated their lives to. My father got cancer, so I took over his quest. We have another chance to stop it, but not until I'm old or dead. The next generation, *our* next generation, has to help."

She paged through the notebook. "Is that why it has future events, because of Jacob's grandfather?"

"Yes, he mapped out times that the machine could be stopped."

"Well, I guess we need to get the next generation started."

Chapter Forty-Eight

Palmdale, California
2044

Anthony sat at his desk in the Skunk Works. He had the only complete set of plans for the Vmax3 drive. No one else had the total image. Each department had only the piece they were responsible for. It would all be assembled by his crew alone, in the end.

He kept looking over the cryptic text by Senator James. *How did he get my phone number? No one outside the plant is supposed to have this.*

The invitation was to a bar at six that night. Anthony smiled to himself. He was going to enjoy this. He had no love for Senator James.

When he arrived, Senator James was sitting next to Phillip Anderson. He sat down next to the two. "When did you get out of prison?" Anthony asked.

Anderson smiled. "Presidential pardon, courtesy of Senator James. He protects the people close to him."

"So, what did you want to see me about?"

"Not so fast," Anderson said. He pulled out a wand and scanned up and down on Anthony's clothes. "He's clean."

"What was that all about?"

James folded his arms and leaned back in his chair. "Just checking for bugs. I don't want anyone listening in to our conversation."

"Oh. Why would that be?"

Scowling, James said, "You know perfectly well why that would be. You have the only complete copy of the Vmax3 drive plans. I have bits and pieces, but you have the whole thing. I'm willing to pay five million for a copy of it."

Anthony stroked back his red hair. "Five million dollars? Wow, that seems like a lot. How on earth would I smuggle the plans out of the factory?"

James slid a phone over to him. "This is an exact duplicate of your phone, only it has a built-in scanner. Once you take a picture of the plans, you destroy the phone."

Picking it up, Anthony turned to Phillip. "Isn't this the same phone you were found holding when you were arrested?"

Phillip shook his head. "New and improved version. It's impossible to trace. Once you take the picture, take the battery out and throw the phone into a dumpster."

"Hmm, how is the five million going to be paid?"

James slipped a piece of paper across the table. "This is your new account in the Caymans. It's fifty thousand in seed money. When we get the plans, I'll put the rest of the money there."

"Five million, just for a few scans of drawings. Wow, you have a deal." He shook their hands.

Arriving home that night, he kissed his wife.

"How did your day go, dear?"

"Well, Sarah Dalton Trumball, I had an interesting talk with Senator James."

Her eyes widened. "Is he wanting the drive?"

"Yes, five million is the offer."

"You can't give it to him. In fact, you must make sure the thing never works." She put her hands on her hips.

"No, I can't do that. I might lose you if the thing never works. If Major Dalton doesn't go back into the nineteen hundreds, then you might never be born. No, I'll send Senator James the wrong plans and put the wrong plans back in the archives, too. The real plans I'll destroy, after the drive is built. Dalton goes back in time, you are born, but they can never build another time machine."

She swallowed. "I think it's too risky. Destroy the plans now. I'll take my chances."

"No. Adalwolf destroyed the plane. In the first timeline, the plane was recovered and with that and the knowledge of the employees here, they were able to recreate the drive. They have no plane this go around. All I have to do is give them the fake plans, disappear, and the two of us can live on a beach sipping umbrella drinks the rest of our lives."

She smiled, "If you're sure it will work."

"I'm sure."

Senator James and Phillip Anderson looked over the plans several months later. They met behind closed doors in the Senator's office.

"Who are we going to get to build this thing?" Anderson asked. "You've pretty well tapped out your supply of funds."

"I do have friends in Russia, who ask no questions. They are wanting certain information from me. If I give it to them, then I can get one of their manufacturers to produce the drive. I have a company in China working on the plane."

"All is set then. We will own history."

Phillip Anderson walked into the office a week later. Senator James screamed, "It doesn't work."

"Anthony gave us the wrong plans?"

"Yes, I had some of the Lockheed people look at it and they say it's nothing like the original. Those plans are who knows where by now."

"Can we look at the other plane to see what's different?"

The senator sat down in behind his desk. "The plane hasn't made it back yet." He flipped open his history book. "It says here, the Holocaust still happened. Dalton failed."

Chapter Forty-Nine

Atlantic Ocean
2044

The boat chugged up and back, with three fishing lines in the water. There were no hooks, just weights to make it look like they were on a fishing charter. There was a large cable with an electrical line out the back of the ship for the side scanning radar. Other than that, the disguise was perfect.

A captain and three crew members were on the boat. Two of the men were in the cabin, monitoring the images of the seafloor. The other was watching to make sure the cables weren't getting tangled. The captain spent most of his time in the flying bridge, steering the ship, but came down once in a while to check the status of the operation.

They'd been doing this for four days now. They had covered all the places that the plane should have come down. Dempsey brought out his laptop again. He was losing faith in his estimates. He had gone over and over the model. The plane had to be here. Right here.

He heard the radio call up to the captain. "Sir, we have the object again, but there's nothing else here."

The captain throttled back on the engines. "Get a fix on it. At least we can dive on that. Maybe it's a piece of it, anyway."

"Yes, Sir."

The boat stopped and the anchor dropped. The captain came down the ladder. "We don't have anything but that one object we keep coming across. I'm sending my men down to take pictures of it. It might be a clue as to what's going on."

A crewmember poked his head out of the hatch. "Sir, that ship that's been shadowing us is approaching fast."

"Start reeling in, gentlemen. Make it look like you have a fish on, if possible," the captain replied.

The ship came quickly in view, bearing down on them.

"Coast Guard. Maybe they think we're smuggling drugs. If they search the ship, they are going to be very curious as to what we're doing," Ross said. His shoulders sagged.

A crewmember on the Coast Guard cutter put a bullhorn up to his mouth. "This is the United States Coast Guard. Prepare to be boarded."

"Looks like we have company," the captain said with a sigh.

The cutter threw lines over and soon the two ships were tied up to each other. Five sailors with full combat gear and guns were soon aboard. The cutter's captain joined them.

"Colonel Ross, General Williams, and Major Dempsey, I have warrants for your arrest."

Dempsey looked over to the other two. *How do they know our names?*

"On what charges?" Williams bellowed.

"Destruction of government property, theft of government property, dereliction of duty and whatever else Senator James can think up." He motioned to two of his men. Soon Dempsey, Williams, and Ross were all sitting on the deck of the Coast Guard ship. All the equipment from the boat was brought over and several of the sailors had donned suits and were diving down onto the object.

"They've been watching us the whole time," Dempsey muttered.

"Yes, and we led them right to what they wanted us to," Ross said.

"How's this all going to end?" Dempsey looked around. The crew members from the boat were brought over, and after the divers returned, the small boat was taken under tow.

"This is the end of the line," Ross replied.

Williams leaned against the bulkhead and closed his eyes.

Dempsey shifted in his seat and watched the land get closer and closer. "I hope they don't find it. They'll use it again and destroy time."

"If the thing was there, we would have found it," Ross said.

"I could be wrong in my model. The ship's logs could have given the wrong latitude and longitude. The plane could be beyond repair. There are endless possibilities."

"Or, someone could have beaten us to the thing. It's been down there a long time."

"None of the charges will stick, especially the dereliction of duty. None of us were on duty at the time," Williams said, his eyes still closed.

On shore, they were all put in the brig then they brought out one at a time for questioning. Dempsey was the last to be escorted into the interview room. An Air Force MP stood guard while General Parker and Senator James sat across from the Major.

"Was this all some type of joke?" Senator James' beady eyes tried to bore holes through him, it seemed.

"I don't know what you mean, Sir."

"You've destroyed information, wiped hard drives, and now you sent us on a wild goose chase. What are you trying to hide?" James' face reddened.

"We were just out hanging around, fishing, Sir."

"With side-scanning sonar and enough sophisticated equipment to make an admiral jealous? I don't think so. What were you looking for? Before you answer that, I want you to know we've already run the model you had on your laptop, so we know you were looking for something."

Dempsey swallowed hard. He didn't know what the others had told them, and he didn't know what was down there. He debated about giving them what they wanted, but he looked the senator in the eyes and remembered how much he hated the man. "We found what we were looking for. That small object we were about to dive on. That was what we were looking for."

The senator sat back in his seat. Dempsey looked at the general. *What's that look?* He wondered. *Is it sympathy?"*

"Take him back to his cell."

"You have the same answer from all three of them. They were looking for the marker. You have no reason to hold them. I am ordering their release," The general said.

"You can't do that. They know where the airplane is. We need to hold them until they confess."

The general was undaunted. He stood up, "Good day, Senator."

An hour later all three of the prisoners had been brought into a conference room, their handcuffs removed. A minute later, General Parker came in. He laid a stack of pictures on the desk. "I don't know if you already know what the marker said, but if you didn't, I brought you pictures of it. All of the made-up charges have been dropped. As for Major Dempsey and Colonel Ross, you are to report to me on next Monday where you'll be reassigned. General Williams, you have a good day." He turned to leave then stopped and faced them one more time. "Gentlemen, you have my sympathies."

Ross looked at the photo. It showed a granite large cross with the inscription, 'Captain Gerald Myers. Born September 15, 2012. Died January 6, 1894.'

Chapter Fifty

New York, New York

2046

Jarvin Musktel, Deputy Director of the CIA, looked at the men and women of his command. He was the head of special projects, which involved spying on Middle East terror groups. Felix Schmidt was among those in the room. It was a quiet group this day. One of their pilots had been shot down. "Ethan Fields, though not a favorite brother, was a brother to all of us. His courage in the face of danger was unmatched. We will miss him. It must never come to light what he was doing when he was shot down. He knew the dangers."

He let the group settle down, before he went on. "Because we have been compromised, this group must be dissolved. Each of you are to be reassigned to other units. It has been a proud moment to serve with you."

Everyone seemed to know that was coming. With little fanfare, they all filed out of the room.

His secretary barged into the room. "Sir, it's the FBI. They want to talk to you."

"Tell them to go away. I'm busy."

A man with close-cropped hair walked into the room. "Sir, I'm Special Agent Carlson with the FBI. I need to ask you a few questions."

The sun was setting over a small Caribbean island. Anthony lay in his hammock reading a book. Sarah brought him out a drink and a cheese on a platter to snack on and sat down beside him. "Do you think Senator James will ever find us?"

"He won't look. He'll send his lap dog, Phillip Anderson, to do the looking."

"I don't like that man." She took some brie off the plate.

"Don't worry, Senator James is very busy right now. He's probably forgotten all about us anyway, with the congressional investigation going on into all those missing funds. He thought a time machine would solve all of his problems, but it just made more for him."

"I did feel guilty about all that money at first." She sipped her drink. "But then I got over it. Our families spent over a hundred years trying to stop that time machine. Now, we've finally done it. It turned out to be a profitable thing to do."

"I'm hoping you have news that can get me out of here. Did you get control of the..." James stopped to look around to make sure the guards were out of earshot. "Well you know what."

"I have no news. There is no trace of that 'machine' anywhere," Ross replied.

James slumped back in the chair. "Then I'm stuck here."

"You always were stuck here. I wasn't about to try to get a plane, that, in my opinion, should never have existed. It doesn't matter, however, no one going to bust you out of jail, in the past or the future."

James smiled, through his depression. "One could only hope. Phillips has a version of it. I just have to wait until he can fix the Vmax3 drive."

"If what Dalton says is true, we won't even know. All this," Ross motioned around the room, "won't even be a distant memory."

"Still, it would have been an awesome thing to have the power to fix everything that's gone bad through time. I figured out how to do it, too. Change the past, then go into the future and see how it works out. If it's better, keep the changes, if not, go back and change it back."

Ross chuckled. "You would have been playing Time God. Deciding who lives and who dies. Now someone else might take up the role and I'm sure they don't have the stellar ethics that you possess."

James gave him a sideways glance. "I was going to get rid of a few annoyances along the way. I suppose you're right. I'm not the man to be making those decisions. Still, Time God does have a ring to it."

Ross glanced down at his watch, "Well, Time God, I have to go. Visiting hours are over." He stood up and motioned for the guard to let him out, then shook James' hand. "Take care of yourself."

"It's only for a little while," James replied.

When Ross finally came through the last of the security gates, Williams was waiting for him in the car. "Why do you bother with the man?"

"You should come in with me one of these days. He looks really good in orange." Ross suddenly realized his motivation. He was briefly disappointed with himself.

"I suppose you're right. I would love to see him in orange. I will come in next time."

Both men laughed.

Chapter Fifty-One

Phillip Anderson stood on the back of the ship looking at the submersible. The thing was huge. It was almost as large as the Vmax3 plane that it was being used to find. The captain of the research vessel walked up to him.

"Beauty, isn't she."

Phillip started at it. It had engines on the tips of the fins. It looked like an alien spaceship. "I wouldn't call her beautiful, but I will say it the most powerful looking submersible I've ever seen."

"I think she's a beauty. She can stay submerged for two weeks at a time with a crew of tow. The sonar and metal detectors are in the pod on the bottom."

"Can we find every piece of metal on the sea floor? It's believed Dalton blew the plane to bits."

"The *Carra May* can find and retrieve even the smallest piece of metal on the sea floor. If it's down there, we'll get it. It will be a massive jigsaw puzzle in the end, with extra pieces. Do you think it's worth it? It's going to take years."

"Yes, I have to get Senator James out of prison. I'll go to a time he isn't in jail, then get rid of his enemies."

"You can do all that with your machine?"

"I just need the Vmax3 drive, then I can do anything."

"Okay, let's do this," the captain smiled.

Two divers boarded the submersible and the ship's crane hoisted it into the ocean. It soon disappeared below the waves.

"There she goes," the captain said. "We've plotted out the currents and the projected debris area. It's a hundred miles long. It will take about a year and a half to get all the bits and parts."

"I guess Senator James will have to cool his heels a little while longer."

When the captain made his way back up to the bridge, the First Mate said, "Isn't this like looking for a needle in the haystack?"

"A million needles and an ocean full of haystacks. If they are missing even one part, it won't work, then the impossible task of putting the thing together when we do give them the parts."

The first mate scratched his head. "Why are we doing this, then?"

"We needed to test out the *Carra May* in all conditions. This way we can do it on Senator James' dime."

The first mate nodded, "I see."

"No, this is the end of the line for James' quest. The tides and currents have spread that machine of his far and wide. Turn on the camera, I want to see what they're doing down there."

Books by Clark Graham

Science Fiction

A Loop in Time

A Hole in Time

A Rift in Time

End of the Innocent

Millennium Man

Nick Spool, Galactic Private Eye

Fantasy

Dwarves of Elvenshore

Lost Cities of Elvenshore

Elf's Bane

The Last of the Minotaur

Curse of the Druid King

War of the Druid King

Dwarves Druids and Dragons

Return of the Druid

Wizards and Heroes

Trouble With Dragons

Children of the Gods

Emily and the Shadow King

Mystery

International Mysteries

Murder Beneath the Palms

Other

Unexpected Tales and Feel Good Stories

Moon Over Mykonos

Etched Upon the Stone

Bullets and Blondes

Sample Chapter

Millennium Man

Chapter 1: Montana

Two Marines stood guard at the door. Director Phillip James walked to the most secure part of the top secret facility. It was deep in the mountains of Montana. Unlike NORAD, that had all sorts of publicity in comparison, this was a small operation. It was built with one single purpose, to support the Millennium Man. The hallway looked just like any hospital hallway in America, clean and white with the slight smell of antiseptic cleaners.

Six foot two, with short brown hair, Phil was slender, a man that most women would consider attractive. Phil walked up to the guards at the door. He was in his white lab coat and carried a clip board. There was so much computer data being used your street clothes had to be covered up at all times by a lab coat. All dust and dirt was to be kept at a minimum both for the health of the man they guarded and the highly sensitive electrical equipment in the complex. The clip board did not have charts and graphs on it like most clip boards of executives. Phil had a bad memory and always carried the clip board to write notes and reminders on.

The building had white cinderblock walls. Drop down florescent lights illuminated the halls and rooms. Every part of the building was cleaned regularly to keep dust at a minimum. Everyone who worked there also lived there, to limit the flow of information that left the complex. Phillip had just left his office and made his way down to where the Millennium Man lived. He had been ill of late and Phil was going to check up on him. It was the only reason he would venture to this part of the building. Otherwise he would gladly stay away.

The Marine guard scanned Phil's badge, although he recognized him. When the machine dinged, the guard nodded his approval and then opened the door for Phil.

The room he entered into was brightly lit and full of medical equipment. Two doctors, five nurses and many medical assistants all stood around the bed of the patient. They had been trying to revive him for two hours. By the time Phil had arrived, they had given up.

The doctor turned to face Phil and just shook his head. "It's over. There is nothing else we can do."

"It can't be over; in this time of terror threats, we need him more than ever," Phil protested.

"He's dead." The doctor walked out of the room followed by most of the nurses and medical assistants.

The other doctor stayed. "Write *this* on your clipboard. Time of death, January 16th at 7:50 pm," he said. He was Rick Allred, the best of the best when it came to medical doctors. Paying his huge salary was not a problem with the United States Government bankrolling the project. He had black hair and stood a couple of inches shorter than Phil. He was getting a slight pot belly, but at fifty -two, he didn't care. He had no family close to him after his last divorce. He had no intention of starting over with another romance.

"What are we going to do?"

"Find the next one. "

Phil didn't know what that meant. He had been hired after the Millennium Man was already here. "How do we do that?"

"Quickly. The Blues are playing god with us. They only make one Millennium Man at a time. Whoever it is, we have to find him and get him here before his powers fully develop."

It was an alien race that they called the Blues. Even though their ships were undetectable by normal radar, the United States had developed a type of pulse radar that picked them up. The blips on the radar turned blue when it detected one of the alien ships. The name had stuck. They had no idea who the Blues were, only that they had the power to turn the human brain into something with telepathic abilities. This greatly enhanced the fight against terror, having someone who could find threats from afar.

The only problem is the Blues only did it to one person at a time, so the agency would find and kidnap that person. They had tried to mimic the alien technology a few times, but it only resulted in the death of the person they transplanted it into. The interface was so intermingled with the brain that massive brain swelling always resulted and death followed shortly after. The aliens had gotten around this somehow.

"What if they don't make another one in the United States?" Phil wanted answers. He was supposed to be the Director of the operation, but he still had a lot to learn. The loss of the Millennium Man had come too soon.

"Let's see, a man that can read everyone else's mind, even from great distances suddenly appeared in the midst of an enemy regime? They would know all of our secrets and every move we were going to make before we made it. It would be a catastrophe. The very thought makes me shudder. We had better hope that they don't do that. They have always made them here in the North America. We had one from Canada once. Kidnapping him in a foreign country and sneaking him across the border was a feat, let me tell you. Hopefully the aliens will pick a younger man this time. We seem to only get twenty years out of the Millennium Men we get, almost to the day."

"I wasn't here when we found the last one. I don't know how to go about it," Phil admitted.

"Any weird newspaper headlines about abductions or UFOs in the sky have to be followed up on in great detail. We have to capture the new Millennium Man before he figures out how to use the new power he is given. Otherwise he will know you are coming and you will never catch up with him."

"When should I start looking?" Phil asked.

Dr. Allred looked down at his watch. "Now. As a matter of fact, I would not be going to bed tonight, if I were you."

Phil got out his clipboard and jotted down a note about looking for UFOs and reported abductions. He then rushed up to his office and turned on his computer and started scanning the internet.

Dr. Allred also went to his office, but instead of scanning the internet he got on the phone and called his friend in the Air Force, General Morgan. "Hi, Fred, you know those blue radar blips that you are not supposed to talk about?"

"Yes?"

"I need you to track them and send me locations for any of them that stopped for more than ten minutes."

There was silence over the phone for a few seconds and then the General said, "He's dead, then?" It wasn't the sound of sadness in his voice, but more of an annoyed sound.

"Yes, he's gone."

"I will send you the data."

Made in the USA
San Bernardino,
CA